Short Cut
to Red River

**Center Point
Large Print**

**This Large Print Book carries the
Seal of Approval of N.A.V.H.**

ॐ श्री गणेशाय नमः

Short Cut
to Red River

○ ○ ○ ○ ○ ○ ○ ○ ○ ○ ○

Noel M. Loomis

Center Point Publishing
Thorndike, Maine

DEDICATED TO
ALICE ARMSTRONG
for services above and
beyond the call of duty

This Center Point Large Print edition
is published in the year 2001 by arrangement with
Golden West Literary Agency.

The text of this Large Print edition is unabridged.
In other aspects, this book may vary from the
original edition. Printed in Thailand. Set in 16-point
Times New Roman type by Bill Coskrey.

ISBN 1-58547-093-7

Library of Congress Cataloging-in-Publication Data

Loomis, Noel M., 1905-
    Short cut to Red River / Noel M. Loomis.-- Large print ed.
    p. cm.
    ISBN 1-58547-093-7 (lib. bdg. : alk. paper)
    1. Large type books. I. Title.

PS3523.O554 S55 2001
813'.54--dc21

2001028490

CONNELLY'S EXPEDITION

This is a novel based on history. It is a matter of record that Dr. Henry Connelly, one of the United States' early merchants in Chihuahua, in 1839 undertook the hazardous trip through the "Comanche-infested" wilderness of West and North Texas, to establish a trade route to short cut the long wagon-trail haul down the Santa Fe Trail from Independence. Its major difficulties were about as represented here.

If Connelly's Expedition had succeeded, it is doubtful that the Texan-Santa Fe Expedition of 1841 would have been undertaken, because it would not have been necessary; without the continent-wide ill feeling that followed the latter event, it is possible the Mexican War would not have occurred, and thus everything south of Oregon and west of Texas might still be Mexican. A large "what-if."

Secondary persons in this story are largely taken from the records: Governor Irigoyen, General Conde, Doctor Jennison, the "French widow of a German druggist," Muke-war-rah the Penateka Comanche chief, Black Deaver the Delaware Indian scout, and many others. Henry Connelly later became governor of New Mexico Territory. James Wiley Magoffin, a fascinating character, was a historic trader on the Santa Fe Trail; the Magoffins were a large and prolific family, and many of the descendants live today in the United States.

The economic and political background of this story is consistent with fact. It is hoped the physical background is accurate and representative.

As in most stories of the frontier, the hard-hitting facts of Connelly's Expedition are dominated by the men who took the impossible in stride. They were heroes for a day and then rode back into the wilderness. Small wonder neurotics usually did not last long in the early Southwest; nobody had time to sit around and commiserate with them.

NOEL M. LOOMIS

Descanso, California
THE LAND OF TRANQUILLITY
November 14, 1957

Chapter 1

It was late afternoon in Chihuahua, and the golden sun of Mexico in March had begun to yield to the night coolness flowing down the great slopes of the Sierra Madres west of town.

From one side of the spacious plaza, the twin spires of Chihuahua's great stone cathedral cast long shadows over the cobblestoned street, the paved walk around the square, and the ornate fountain in the middle.

In the stone wall of the cathedral a deep niche housed a statue of St. Matthew, and in the deeper shadows at the foot of the statue an old *pordiosera* waited quietly and inconspicuously. A two-wheeled *carreta* lumbered by slowly, pulled by two oxen who did not like the uneven footing offered by the rounded granite stones. The owner of the *carreta,* a Mexican peon without shoes, walked on the far side, chattering to the bulls, shaming them for their efforts as a matter of course. The cart was empty, and bounced so much it seemed that even the sun-dried strips of rawhide would not be enough to hold it together. As a sort of accompaniment to the peon's not unmusical comments, the ungreased cottonwood axles creaked intermittently. Had the cart been loaded, the wood would have screeched and groaned. But it was empty, and the owner was heading toward the Nueve Gatos—the Nine Cats saloon; perhaps he had delivered a load of corn to the mines—even to Santa Eulalia, eighteen miles east—and now was preparing to spend the income on pulque. Otherwise, he would have been silent.

The beggar woman stepped out quickly and scanned the street. She drew her black *rebozo* close about her face, then shrank again into the shadows. She knew from the sounds to the south that the bullfight was over, and that presently the *ricos* would be along; she would choose her opportunities with care, provided the padre did not see her first. The new priest, who was young, would chide her severely for what she was planning.

She heard a heavy rumbling, the sound of iron tires on the cobblestones, and risked another look.

Governor Irigoyen's great European-made carriage, pulled by five mules, had just driven into the square. She shrank back again, for she had got a silver peso from the governor on his way to the *corrida,* and she knew that the driver or the footman would scold her if she tried again so soon. There was, of course, no possibility of disguising herself.

The governor's carriage clattered past. It had curtains at the windows to keep out the stares of the curious, and it was said it cost more than a thousand *carretas*—but then he was the governor, and a very rich man.

Now she heard shod hoofs on the stones, and knew the sound could mean only one thing: a party of *ricos* from the Peralta rancho, for Don Fidel Peralta was the only man in the state of Chihuahua who shod his horses. That applied only to the horses that he kept for special guests to ride into town; but the auguries were good, for her granddaughter Anita, who worked at the

Peralta ranch, had told her of the great *hombre de campo,* with broad shoulders, lithe body, and eyes quick and observant but sober, who had recently arrived from Nueva Orleans.

The *pordiosera* snickered silently. Anita, in spite of having had three children by three men, was still young, and looked at every man with eyes of love. But he probably was old and leathery, this *rico* from Nueva Orleans. She could only hope that Don Fidel himself was not along, for Don Fidel had known her from his childhood and would be stingy with his *limosna,* in spite of her appearance; whereas the younger men, temporarily shocked and embarrassed, might, in order to play the *gran hombre* before their guest, by accident throw her a gold piece instead of a peso.

She saw them coming—four men on the great black Peralta horses. Her old eyes could not make out their faces, but she was hopeful. She loosened the *rebozo,* dropped it onto her shoulders, then left the niche and walked westward to be in the sunlight so that the sore would show. It covered the upper half of the left side of her face; if exposed long enough to the sun, it dried, cracked, and bled a little. The ancient *curandera* at Santa Eulalia had guaranteed to cure it for her, but the *pordiosera* was no fool. The sore had made her the most successful beggar in Chihuahua for twenty years.

The four riders were still fifty feet away as she waited at the edge of the shadow thrown by the church. The cooler air swept around her, reminding her that her blood was no longer as thick as Anita's. She glanced westward, toward the tremendous mountains that

9

seemed to stretch up and up to the sky. She had been there just once in her lifetime—when she was small and the Apaches had killed all of her family but her. She remembered little except that she had been hungry and that there were great cliffs that no man could climb, and great canyons gouged out by furious cloudbursts.

The governor's carriage had turned up a dirt side street, and the only noise was that made by the hoofs of the four horses. In a few moments the town would be buzzing with talk of the *corrida,* in hovels as well as in the governor's palace, but at that moment the only indication of activity was the sound of tortillas being slapped and shaped, for this was the time of afternoon when the *señoras* with their quick, competent, olive-skinned hands began to prepare the corn cakes for supper. Suddenly the serenity of Chihuahua was broken by the harsh "*¡Sangre! ¡Sangre! ¡Sangre!*" of a crow flying out of a steeple of the cathedral.

The *pordiosera* watched it for a moment, hesitant. "Blood! Blood! Blood!" it cried, frightening the *pordiosera* for a moment, for perhaps the sound was an omen. Well she knew this peaceful square could erupt without warning into violence, bloodshed, and death. It would last but briefly, and then the countryside would be quiet again, and there would be only the wailing of mourners, the masses to be said for the dead, the fees to be paid the priest—so many *reales* for ringing the small bells, more for ringing the big bell, still more for holy water. . . .

More often the peon shrugged and spent his hard-earned copper *clacos* for pulque or mescal, and went on a prolonged drunk. This had its virtues, and was far cheaper than a formal burial. There was still the embarrassing presence of the body, but eventually it would be disposed of. Then the ancient city would settle down again, and no one would hurry or worry, or be concerned about anything.

She saw that all of the men on the horses were young, and was pleased. Apolinar Peralta, son of Don Fidel, who was related to Governor Irigoyen, was leading them—a tall, brown, handsome young man, resplendent in black trousers with flaring legs and green silk inserts set off by silver *conchas,* a red silk sash around his waist, a very white shirt, and the short, embroidered *chaqueta* worn in place of a coat by Mexican horsemen. The *pordiosera* breathed deeply. Give her back fifty years . . .

Beside him was Andrés Vigil, grandson of the customs collector at Matamoros, and beyond him was Hermenijildo Zamora. Don Hermenijildo was a little slimmer and perhaps of a more serious turn than the others, though his age was the same and his love of ostentation equal to theirs.

The man on the opposite side of Don Andrés was a great question in all of Chihuahua. His name was Ed Mangum, and it was said he was a good man to have in front of you. He was dressed like the young *ricos* and his skin was as brown as theirs, but he was an obvious Anglo trying to act like a Mexican. It was Mangum who rode the chestnut, and the beggar recognized it as one of José Cordero's horses. She noted the fact, for Cordero was known to have invested heavily in goods

11

to be brought down the Santa Fe Trail from San Luis, and Mangum was a trader and wagon-train man.

They were almost even with her when the *pordiosera* loosened the scarf on her shoulders and scuttled crab-fashion into the street. As she met young Peralta, she held up a wrinkled brown hand with fingers deformed by rheumatism, while on the side opposite the sore she shaded her eyes with the other hand. The joints of both hands were enlarged and twisted, and she made sure this would be noticeable.

"*¿Señores?*"

She kept her old voice querulous, watching the four, studying, weighing. The fifth man, the one from Nueva Orleans, was behind the others, and as the three young Mexicans pulled up their horses in momentary astonishment she was aware that Mangum had pulled to one side, aloof and cynical, while the fifth stayed back, watching.

She saw at once why Anita could not cease talking about the *hombre de campo*. It was not the way he sat the saddle—erect but somehow easy and relaxed—nor the half-smile on his face—neither overimpressed nor unfriendly—but the look of his eyes and the set of his jaw, which together spoke of self-confidence and determination. She noted with interest that he made no attempt to be a Mexican *rico*, but wore conventional Anglo broadcloth and a beaver hat.

She turned her eyes again to Apolinar and advanced a step with her crooked hand held high. "*Por mis niños, señor, que no tienen leche.*"

Apolinar's horse walked sidewise, his head tossing,

the heavy silver on the bridle gleaming in the sun. Apolinar partially recovered, and tossed her a coin. It was only a peso, but she picked it deftly out of the air.

Mangum said cynically: "She's too old to have babies. She's gray-haired. Anyway, neither she nor her descendants ever drank a cup of milk. She'll spend that money on pulque."

Apolinar glanced at him, apparently embarrassed to have been caught by such a trick; but Hermenijildo, who was said to have married a niece of General Conde, observed, "As long as we have our brandy, why should the beggars be deprived either of milk or of pulque?"

Andrés glanced at the fifth man. "How is it in Boston or New Orleans, *señor?*"

"Not much different," Ross Phillips said thoughtfully.

"It is a great problem in all of Méjico," said Andrés. He alone, of the three young Mexicans, had a neat black mustache, waxed at the ends, and he was a little heavier than the others, though he was the youngest. He spoke somewhat pompously for a young man. "All we can do is toss the *limosna.*" He shrugged. "It is a thing of Méjico." And with that, he seemed to dismiss it from his mind.

The *pordiosera* was looking the five men over shrewdly from beneath her misshapen hand to see if there might be additional alms, but the man on the chestnut horse seemed to have squelched any further generosity. She started to turn away, but the man from New Orleans moved his arm. She caught the gleam of a gold piece, and snatched it, murmuring, *"Gracias."*

She saw the puzzled looks on the faces of the three *ricos* as they considered Mangum's words and Phillips' action; then she scuttled back to the front of the church and disappeared in the shadows.

Apolinar swung his horse around, led the way onward, and in a few clattering steps the group had recovered its poise. For this was Chihuahua in the spring of 1839, and there was little to do but eat, sleep, go to the *corridas* or the cockfights, inspect their estates, and make love—which latter was, after all, the only worthwhile occupation.

Phillips' horse lagged, but that suited him, for it gave him a chance to observe Mangum. Phillips was deeply tanned; his hair was also brown and he wore long, well-trimmed sideburns. From his obvious Anglo coloring he was known to the Mexicans as a *güero*. Such light-complected ones were popular among Mexican women—a fact which had led him into two duels in Zacatecas the summer before. His dress was very plain except for a white brocaded waistcoat.

The patting of hands on tortilla dough began to arise from all directions now as the sounds from the Alameda south of the plaza indicated that the *corrida* was over and that the *hombres* would presently finish their pulque and excited talk and come home for supper. Somewhere a chicken squawked suddenly as a busy *señora* kicked it out of the living room.

"¡Qué bonito día!" exclaimed Andrés, obviously wanting to change the mood. "And what a beautiful selection of bulls!"

"The fourth fight," said Hermenijildo fervently, "was perfection."

Apolinar looked back at Ross. "I felt sorry for Arellano, on his last bull. Nine swords! *¡Qué lástima!*"

"Why pity him?" Mangum said sourly. "He got paid for it."

Ross had been looking ahead to the balcony of the Sierra house, half a block from the plaza. Chihuahua was a neat town, with streets running square with the compass, and most of the houses were of one story; but the Sierra house was prominent, being two stories high at the front, as befitted the residence of a former military commander of the state, now dead.

Andrés said cautiously, "Perhaps he did look clumsy."

"I don't think so," said Phillips. "I've seen Arellano fight in Querétaro, and he has always performed ably. I shouldn't wonder if there was something wrong with the bull today. I daresay they found that a deformed shoulder blade kept the sword from slipping through."

"I say he's clumsy!" Mangum said sharply.

Phillips was astonished at the belligerence in Mangum's face, but he looked away.

A pig scurried across the street, and after it came four small, black-eyed, barefooted children, shouting shrilly. They crossed in front of the horses, and Apolinar pulled up the black for a moment. They were near the corner of the plaza and the Sierra house, and Ross pulled gently back on the reins, visualizing the action of the spade bit against the roof of the stallion's mouth.

A curious sequence of events had brought Mangum into their company. Ross, who was staying at Apolinar's father's ranch, had got along with the three Mexicans like brothers, although he was a few years older, and Don Fidel had suggested they take in the *corrida* to see the great Arellano. The four had ridden in from Los Saucillos and found General Conde in a carriage with a broken wheel. They had given him a lift to his home where he had insisted they stop for a glass of brandy. Cordero, an older man, had suggested that the four younger ones take his guest, Mangum, with them to the fight, since he was new in Chihuahua—and there had been no polite way to decline.

Mangum had not been a pleasant member of the party. He seemed ready to argue about every point that came up and to disagree with them—especially Ross. Now, Ross reflected, if they could dispose of Mangum courteously they might yet end the affair with a fitting celebration. There were parties—

"I said raise your hat, you *burro!*"

Ross realized with a start that the words were addressed to him. He noted the hostility in the cold, gray-blue eyes, and glanced around at the Mexicans.

They were curvetting their stallions, their great black hats in their hands. As Ross glanced up at the balcony, he saw Valeria Sierra standing there. She was a pure Castilian blonde, a rare type in northern Mexico, and the sun shone through her white lace mantilla and made her hair gleam like sun on water. The black had taken him almost under the balcony; he stood up in his stirrups, raised his heavy beaver hat, and looked straight into her dark eyes. Her smile was evidence that she recognized him. He swept the hat before him in a great arc, then turned abruptly toward Mangum and swung the hat backhanded with all his strength.

It crashed against the right side of Mangum's head. For a moment the man seemed to be stunned. His big hand went to his face and he shook his head briefly. Then his eyes became hard. "You know I'll kill you for that," he said coldly.

"That's a matter of opinion." Ross spun his crushed hat into the street. "And of ability," he added.

Mangum stiffened, but his voice was controlled. "My seconds will call on you this evening."

Ross, his hands resting on the big Spanish saddlehorn, said: "Such rigamarole is unnecessary. We're both Anglos. We can settle it now."

The three young Mexicans drew around them silently, apprehensively. Ross glanced up at the balcony. Valeria was watching, but when she saw his eyes on her she turned quickly and went inside, her full skirt swirling.

"We shall fight as gentlemen—not ruffians," Mangum said harshly.

Ross, his eyes half closed, looked again at Mangum. "Fighting is fighting," he said. "It's up to you."

"My seconds will choose the time and place. You will have the choice—"

"I know the rules," Ross said sharply.

Whatever else he was, Mangum wasn't a bluffer. "Very well," he said stiffly, and without a word or a look for any of them he wheeled the chestnut and rode off at a gallop.

Ross raised his eyebrows. "A very unceremonious leavetaking."

Apolinar said quickly: "*Señor,* allow me to offer my earnest regrets. I personally am distressed, and I know the governor will be distressed to learn that a man who is practically a guest of the state has been challenged to a duel on his third day in Chihuahua."

Ross replied: "It's obvious the man has been looking for trouble ever since we met him. But why?" He looked sharply at the three.

All shook their heads solemnly.

"Then why did Señor Cordero ask you to take him with us?"

"Don José is my godfather," said Andrés.

Ross frowned. "But why did Mangum concentrate his ill humor on me? It could not have been personal, so it must have been—of course, it was business!"

"But you've never had dealings with him," protested Hermenijildo.

"No. No, I haven't; but I have a feeling I shall—in the future."

Andrés said, with some anxiety, "He is said to have killed a number of duelists at Acapulco."

Apolinar said sharply to Andrés: "Watch out for the heels of the black! That stud has marked up every horse that was ever pastured with him."

Andrés moved around.

"Mangum seems to feel the need of practice," said Ross. "What does he fight best with?"

"Pistols, they say."

"Very well, I shall choose six-shooters. Would one of you care to be my second?"

All three spoke together.

"One is enough," said Ross. He looked at Hermenijildo, who was a year or two older than the others, and appeared reliable. "If it isn't too much trouble," Ross said apologetically.

Hermenijildo's voice was grave. "It will be an honor."

Almost as one man the four wheeled the blacks to the south in the direction of Los Saucillos. But a woman's voice stopped them as they leaned forward in their huge old Spanish saddles:

"¡Señores! ¡El sombrero fino!"

Ross stopped the black on its haunches, turned it, and looked down. A young Mexican woman stood with his big beaver in one hand. She was not shading her eyes nor frowning nor squinting into the sun, and she wore the usual low-necked white blouse—spotlessly clean, for no matter what the circumstances, a Mexican woman always managed to have a clean blouse. She was in her early twenties, bare-legged, and wore home-made moccasins. Her glossy black hair was drawn neatly to the back of her neck, and somehow, in spite of a heavy baby in one arm, she managed to look graceful and pretty, though she wasn't over five feet tall. Three more children of stair-step ages hung to her red skirt, and a little behind her, leading a burro piled with some mysterious cargo, was her husband, about the same age, and also pleasantly clean.

Ross, noting the ragged condition of their clothing,

reached in his pocket for a silver *tostón;* but the woman said quickly. "We are not *pordioseros, señor.*"

Ross, momentarily undecided, looked at the man, who was hardly older than Apolinar but who wore a handsome mustache, the more notable because the left side of it was glossy black, the right snow white. "We are happy to be of service to you, *señor,*" he said.

"How are you called?" asked Ross.

"Diego Olivarez, *señor,* but I am sometimes called"—the peon smiled broadly—"*Bigote Doblado*—Double Mustache."

Ross bowed slightly. "I should like—"

"No, *señor.*" Diego was pleasant but firm, and Ross liked his look of capability and self-assurance—pride, perhaps, that was too often lacking in the peons.

The woman moved nearer and held the hat up. He took it, noting that she had brushed it for him. "*Mil gracias, señora.* What is your name?"

"I am Carlota, wife of Diego."

"I know him," Apolinar said in a low voice. "He worked for Olivarez until he paid off his father's debt."

"He's not a relative of Olivarez then?"

"Not legally." Apolinar shrugged. "He might be so by blood. Who knows? Sometimes the Indian slave girls had babies without husbands—this was before slavery was abolished—and they usually adopted the name of the owner. Now, of course, there is no slavery—"

"Only legal bondage," said Ross.

Apolinar shrugged again. "It is the law."

"Where do you live?" asked Ross.

She pointed northeast.

"In the desert?" he asked.

"Across the desert."

"It is a long way to come to trade."

"We don't come often—twice a year."

He held out a gold coin. "Please take this—for the *niños*."

Her answer was dignified. "No, *señor*. We have all we need—a place to live, the *niños*"—she glanced down at them proudly—"plenty of game to eat, sunshine to keep us warm, the stars at night—"

"You could buy coffee with this."

"We will buy coffee with the skins Diego has on the jack."

"Sugar, then."

"There is wild honey for the gathering." She backed away two or three steps.

Ross put the hat on firmly. "I am under great obligation to you, *señora*," he said.

"It is nothing," she answered.

"Good luck to you both," he said, and turned the black.

They rode in silence through the town. Gradually the tension left Ross, and he became aware of the steady plopping of the hoofs, the ubiquitous and comforting domesticity of hands shaping tortillas, the sudden and almost disconcerting squawk of a chicken, the intermittent yapping of dogs, the cries of children racing in the dusty streets.

There were no sidewalks. The roadway extended from wall to wall of the houses, which were without

21

porches or indented entrance ways. The windows were tiny because of the expensiveness of glass, and many of them were covered with sheets of split mica or even with oiled deerskin. Only the deep-set windows gave any indication of the great thickness of the brown adobe; otherwise the walls were flush and straight, and one house joined another. Occasionally, on the second story that marked the *casa* of a well-to-do family, there appeared a tiny wrought-iron balcony. From the edges of the flat roofs the ends of peeled cottonwood logs extended for a foot beyond the walls.

The sun was lower, nearing the ridge of the Sierra Madres. The edge was gone from the jauntiness of the three *caballeros*. Hermenijildo had become very sober, as befitted the second of a man who might well be dead within twelve hours; Andrés seemed frightened, and Apolinar concerned, for Ross was the guest of his uncle the governor—not to mention the fact, well known to them all, that Ross's mission was semidiplomatic and very important economically to the state and to the city of Chihuahua and its merchants.

Ross rode along easily. Now that the first impact of the challenge was over, he found himself thoughtful but calm. Fighting duels seemed always to be a part of his business, but he had hardly anticipated that when he had come to lead the train; primarily he had been pleased that he would have an opportunity to be near Valeria.

They rode in silence, crossing the aqueduct that brought water to Chihuahua. The adobes were scattered now. A donkey looking out of a front door stretched his neck upward in a raucous bray. They left the town with its dusty streets and irrigation canals, and struck out across the prairie, following a trail well beaten into the sparse grass of the dry soil. The shadows down the mountains were very long, and the great slopes were hidden in a twilight haze.

"Fine horses," Ross said.

Andrés nodded. "Don Fidel has bred nothing but black horses for thirty years."

Apolinar nodded. "Papá has thousands—all beautiful."

A mile past the aqueduct Andrés turned off. "I am expected at home before the *baile* tonight," he said, and added, half humorously, half wryly, "No doubt Papá will have some instructions for my proper conduct."

Apolinar laughed shortly. "Is his concern for you or for the *señoritas?*"

Andrés lifted his eyebrows. With his mustache he was a very handsome and very engaging young man. "I think his chief worry is for the foreigners." He glanced at Ross. "With the Magoffins and Connelly, and Dr. Jennison, and Adolf Speyer, and Señor Mangum and Señor Phillips—" He shrugged. "The commerce of Chihuahua is being overrun with Anglos, to hear him tell it."

Ross studied his horse's ears. "There *are* a lot of us." He looked up. "But most of the money is put up by Mexican merchants."

"Papá says men like Magoffin and Wiley are becoming much too well intrenched. However, that isn't his real concern."

Apolinar leaned over to rub his horse's neck. "To tell the truth, Don Mauricio is worried about the younger generation," he said. "The Mejicanos stay home and do the bookkeeping while the Anglos get in the saddle and take the caravans through Indian country, and Don Mauricio feels that the Mexican race is losing its vigor." He laughed. "You wouldn't think so, from the squadrons of *niños* that spring up each year."

Andrés raised a hand. "I'll see you tonight," he said, and put the black into a far-ranging lope, for the Vigil ranch was three leagues into the mountains.

Hermenijildo, sitting back quietly, said with gravity, "If you don't mind, Apolinar, I'll stay at your place until the duel is over—since I am Don Ross's second."

"By all means." Apolinar saw that Ross was looking back at the town, and turned his horse alongside. Hermenijildo noted their movements, but did not join them.

The sun was over the western range of the mountains, seemingly balanced on the top of the ridge, sending long streamers of yellow light across the wild, rugged slopes and lighting up the pine-covered ridges, but leaving the valleys dark and mysterious like Mexico herself. The last sunlight lit up the town of Chihuahua, now to their northeast, lying in a crescent-shaped flat in the mountains.

Beyond the town, to the north, mule trains and ox-cart caravans, as well as the heavy-laden wagons of the far-traveling, hard-booted men from Independence, came with merchandise that tripled and quadrupled in value by virtue of making the two-thousand-mile trip from Independence across plains swept by Comanches and through mountains infested with Apaches. As Ross watched the sun play on the bare brown peaks beyond the town, he thought that, with luck, profitable trade would soon be traveling a different road, and new fortunes would be made on the hazard of a single trip. His own would be among them.

He gazed absently at the town itself. The churches stood out in quiet dignity, with the twin steeples of the cathedral towering over all, and from somewhere came the mellow tolling of a bell. He noted the wide, straight streets at right angles, the shining white of the houses of the *ricos,* the spots of green provided by the budding cottonwoods. At last he turned to Apolinar. "A pretty town," he commented.

Apolinar nodded. "I like it, except when the Apaches come."

Ross glanced back at Hermenijildo as they rode off. Young Zamora was taking his duties as second very seriously; he hadn't smiled since the incident in the street.

Two hours later they turned in at the big gate of Los Saucillos, the Peralta ranch, about dark. The brand was burned in the gateposts, but Ross hadn't figured out yet what it was; he suspected it had started out as a capital *P* with flourishes, but somewhere a cross or two had been added, and perhaps a royal crest, and now it was truly a "*¿Quién Sabe?*" brand.

The usual pack of dogs came to meet them, and Apolinar ordered them back to the house. A man rode from a clump of willows along the creek, followed by a servant on a mule.

"Don Fidel," said Ross.

"*¡Señor!*" Don Fidel Peralta looked at them keenly. He glanced at his son Apolinar, then scrutinized Hermenijildo's sober face. "So! There is trouble, no? *Señoritas,* yes?"

Because Apolinar did not reply immediately, Ross spoke up. "It is hard to say, Don Fidel, what exactly *is* at the bottom of it."

Peralta's black eyes narrowed. He was a fierce-looking man with swarthy, pockmarked skin and a black mustache at least a foot wide. "Then it wasn't one of these *muchachos*. It must have been you, Don Ross." His eyes narrowed. "From the tragic look on Hermenijildo's face, you have been challenged and he is your second."

Ross rested his hands on the saucer-sized saddlehorn and looked up. "Maybe you can tell me who has challenged."

Peralta paused. "You haven't been here long enough to get involved in politics. I would judge it was economic."

"Señor Mangum," Apolinar said shortly, unable longer to restrain himself.

There was a quick lift of Peralta's heavy black eyebrows. "So? Señor Mangum."

Apolinar explained. "We were before Señorita Sierra's house, and—"

"With the *señorita* on the balcony, of course."

"*Por supuesto,*" said Ross.

Peralta smiled, and nodded to Apolinar to continue.

"Unaccountably, Señor Mangum seemed to take offense because Don Ross did not take off his hat as soon as the rest of us."

"I had met her in Durango," Ross said, "and I was thinking she was as beautiful as before."

Peralta nodded wisely.

"He insulted Don Ross, and—"

"I nearly unseated him with my hat," said Ross, adding speculatively, "I'd always wondered if it could be done."

"And the answer is no?"

Ross bowed apologetically. "I tried very hard."

Peralta nodded absently. "It is perhaps no surprise, but one wonders why he chose that particular time and place."

"To appear important in the eyes of the *señorita,*" said Apolinar quickly.

Peralta's glance was sharp. "Perhaps you *muchachos* know more about life than Don Mauricio suspects. You are most likely right. Does Señor Mangum, then, have calf's eyes at the *señorita*—and, if so, for herself or for her fortune?"

"Doña Valeria's father and Papá were 'brothers,' " Apolinar explained. "They were in partnership, and half of Los Saucillos still belongs to her."

"It doesn't matter," Peralta said. "There's enough for all. There are thousands of acres and forty-five thousand horses."

Ross observed, "A man marrying into the family might force a division."

Peralta considered. "Whatever it is, you may be

sure that Mangum is serious about it, as he is about everything."

Ross leaned over and straightened the brow-band of the bridle. "What is he doing in Chihuahua?"

"I am told that Cordero sent for him."

"For what purpose?" asked Ross.

"Mangum is well experienced at moving goods over difficult trails. He has worked all over Mexico and South America."

Ross looked up sharply. "Connelly and Magoffin and a dozen others know every league of the Santa Fe Trail."

"They do," said Don Fidel, "and so it is obvious that Cordero is not spending a large amount of money to have Mangum find the way to Independence."

"That leaves—"

"Exactly what it seems to leave, Don Ross. Cordero has heard of our plans—actually there has been no secret about them—and he has employed Mangum to be sure we are not successful in establishing a trail across Texas."

"Why is that necessary?" asked Ross. "There is room for all."

"Not if you are already committed in Independence or St. Louis, *señor*. It may even be that Cordero's operating money comes from that end of the Santa Fe Trail, and if he were to change his route he might lose that backing."

Ross smiled. "I thought all Chihuahua merchants were wealthy."

"Since the panic," Don Fidel said, "we never know

who is poor and who is rich. It is worth noting that Cordero has not offered to come in with us on the Texas venture."

"That means he can't afford to lose."

"Exactly. I know he has a caravan leaving Independence in May; the goods for it are already bought, so . . ." He shrugged.

Ross said thoughtfully, "Then the verdict is that Mangum has been brought here to stop the Texas expedition, and he has already taken the first step by challenging me to a duel."

"With obvious assurance that he will win it," said Don Fidel.

Ross smiled. "If he loses, he won't collect his fee."

Don Fidel looked worried. "You are not afraid, *señor?*"

Ross took off his heavy beaver and examined it carefully. One edge was bent where it had struck Mangum's face. He brushed the hat with his sleeve as the horse broke into a lope. "It seems to me," he said, raising his voice over the rhythmic swish of the horse's hoofs in the deep grass of the meadow, "that I am well armed." He put the hat back on his head, looked at Peralta, and smiled.

Chapter 2

The open meadow was still fairly light and gave a good view of the Los Saucillos headquarters, which was like a small town. Don Fidel's home

29

was a large adobe of two stories, built like a hollow square, with the center, the *placeta,* used to protect the animals, and various rooms around the outside arranged for fighting off an attack. Around this main building and out to a distance of three hundred yards were scattered at random the one-room adobe huts of the peons. Prominent among them was a small church, square and flat like the other buildings but distinguished by a cross on top.

The four men rode into the scattered cluster of huts. A fifteen-year-old mother with a baby on her hip was shooing two scrawny chickens into the hut for the night, and she paused to stare at them. One of the black stallions, Ross knew, was worth many times the entire value of such a family's possessions, including their hut and their clothing and whatever assorted barnyard animals they might claim. Dogs ran out yapping, but retreated when they heard Peralta's voice. A barefooted young man of eighteen, wearing the peon's big straw hat and a soiled white shirt with a collar-band, fingered a battered guitar and sang a sad song of love and passion unrequited:

> " 'O my *chiquita,* have pity on me,
> A poor vaquero
> Whose heart is at your feet.' "

Apolinar said briefly. "He's at it again."

"He sounds heartbroken," Ross observed.

Peralta snorted. "That's Plácido's special talent. He's the most persuasive lover between Chihuahua and

Durango—and only a billy goat is more democratic in his taste." He added. "He's also one of the best mule men in northern Mexico."

"Who is the girl this time?"

"Anita—a servant girl of Papá's. She must be working in the kitchen just now."

Near the church a Franciscan priest was watering nasturtiums, bright with an abundance of yellow, orange, and red blossoms. He straightened, bareheaded, brown-robed, and with only sandals on his feet.

"Good evening, Father Ramón," said Peralta.

The priest smiled. *"Buenas noches."* He noted Hermenijildo. "How is your wife, my son?"

"Very good, Father."

"No *niños* yet?"

Hermenijildo said, rather shortly, "Not yet."

The priest observed the note of tension in Hermenijildo's voice, and said, "There is time," and went back to his watering.

They rode through a large opening in the big house, past massive gates tied back with rawhide, into a large courtyard. Peralta dismounted, and servants ran forward to take the horses. The patio was enclosed on all four sides by the building, and within the square were stables, blacksmithing equipment, two wagons, a great clumsy coach for the ladies on state occasions, and a well with stone sides and a bucket hanging from a rope. They were well fortified against attack.

"Let the horses roll," Peralta told the grooms. "Give them some old corn and turn them into the meadow. Remember—*old* corn." He spoke to Ross as they walked across the yard to the left side of the building. "Last week," he said with disgust, "one of the fools fed new corn to a three-year-old mare, and when I took her out for a ride into the mountains next day she died fifteen miles from home and left me afoot!"

There was no more to be said. A man afoot was no man at all in this country of great distances.

"Now," said Peralta, stopping at the hand-hewn cottonwood door of Ross's room, "Connelly and Magoffin will be here presently to look you over and see if they want to risk a quarter of a million dollars in gold and silver to your care."

Ross nodded. "Naturally."

"We'll have dinner when you're ready." Peralta turned abruptly to Hermenijildo. "And you, since you are acting as the *señor's* second, you'd better room with him tonight—though he probably can take care of himself." He turned to Ross with a twinkle in his eye. "From Hermenijildo's manner, one would think this a serious business."

Ross looked at Hermenijildo, and knew how the young man felt. "It may be that," he said quietly.

"*¡Caray!*" Peralta was impatient. "With such an important venture ahead of us, we have no time for play. The welfare of the entire northern half of Mexico depends on the outcome of this expedition."

Apolinar spoke from behind them. "Papá, this *is* serious. He has been challenged by Señor Mangum."

Peralta snorted. "Well—pleasure before business, I suppose." He glanced at them all and said thoughtfully, "This is a big event in a young man's life: a challenge, a duel." He lifted his black eyebrows. "Life or death. I was young myself," he said reminiscently, and then his eyes narrowed. "But remember, all of you—you most of all, Señor Ross—a duel can be fought every day in the week, but a chance to make a fortune comes once in a lifetime."

He stamped off, obviously annoyed at the whole situation.

Apolinar smiled stiffly at Ross. "Don't mind Papá. He believes in making money—but in the next breath he, like Don Mauricio, will be moaning because the younger generation is not man enough to stand on its own feet."

As Ross started into his room he heard Peralta's boots as the don turned. "It's not that we lack vigor in our own race," Fidel snapped, "but our young men do their riding inspecting their estates, and they do their fighting behind a guitar."

Ross looked full at him. "I find it difficult to believe, Don Fidel, that your vigor has not been passed on to your sons."

Peralta looked keenly at him. "So you are a diplomat as well!" He turned on his heel and strode away.

Apolinar chuckled. "Another speech like that, and Papá will adopt you."

Ross grinned. "I would not wish to further complicate my life," he said, and pushed through the door.

He threw his heavy hat on the pallet in one corner, hung his coat and waistcoat on pegs, and prepared to wash in the silver bowl. Suddenly he turned on Hermenijildo. "Don't stand there like Hidalgo's monument! Aren't you hungry?"

"*Señor,* I cannot take this lightly."

"Is this your first time as a second?"

"*Sí.*"

Ross plunged his hands into the tepid water. "You have full authority," he said, splashing his face. "Receive the challenge, name the weapons—six-shooters—and agree on a time and place." He looked around, toweling his face briskly. "Now get ready for dinner!"

They gathered around a massive table in a room lighted by candles. There were only men at the table, for Mexican women did not eat with the men, and Ross readied himself for the endless *platicando* that accompanies any sort of Mexican transaction. For food there was not the omnipresent *guisado* or stew of the *pobres,* but a first course of wine and, later, chicken, pork, and beef, followed by sweet cakes and coffee. At that point the faint chorus of barking dogs came to them through the night air.

Peralta, dropping a piece of brown sugar in his coffee, looked up. "Confounded dogs! I can always tell when we have friendly company, for the dogs are bold. Let an Apache show his head over yonder hill, and the dogs slink into hiding."

"It's not the dogs' fault, Papá," said Apolinar. "They are not trained."

Peralta glared at him. "What do you suggest—a full-time dog trainer?"

Apolinar flushed and looked down at the table. Obviously the canine birth rate precluded any thought of training. "It has to be endured," Peralta growled, "but not liked."

He arose and went into the courtyard and to the big cottonwood gates, which now were closed and barred. Ross, Apolinar, and Hermenijildo went with him. Peralta swung a peephole cover up and looked out. "*¿Quién es?*" he called in a ringing voice.

Above the dogs' yapping came an unruffled answer. "Santiago Magoffin and Enrique Connelly!"

It was now thoroughly dark, and two servants hurried up with blazing torches of sotol stalks. They slid the three log bars out of their keepers and swung the gates wide. A tall man on a dun mule rode into view. In the sputtering yellow light his sloping shoulders gave the impression of great strength. He had large ears, a high forehead, a generous, well-formed nose, and a straight, firm mouth. His gray eyes singled out Ross Phillips at once, and for a moment he scrutinized him. Ross felt that he had been examined minutely, but he did not know the man's conclusion. Then Magoffin swung down from the saddle of his mule and said, "Don Fidel, it is good to see you."

They embraced. Magoffin was not dressed like a Mexican, but wore a long, somber-hued coat, a shirt collar that stood up around his neck, and a wide black tie looped in a large bow.

Dr. Connelly dismounted. He was similarly dressed, but very different in appearance—stocky of build, with square shoulders, rather deep lines alongside his nose, and eyes narrowed as if he had been much in the wind and sun.

35

Peralta took them both into the *sala,* and Ross and the boys followed. After his visitors were seated, Peralta poured brandy. "Cigars?"

"Later," said Connelly.

"Thanks," Magoffin said. "My years on the Trail taught me to prefer a chew."

"Well, gentlemen!" Peralta looked around at the three young men, who stood patiently near the door. Don Fidel was in high good humor. "*Señores,* here is the man you have been waiting to see. It is my pleasure to introduce Señor Ross Phillips, and I am assured by the Mexican Consulate of New Orleans that if any man can take a caravan through the Texas Comanches, this man can."

Connelly studied him over his brandy. "Looks young to me."

Magoffin chuckled. "That's why you and I aren't trying it on our own. We're too old."

"I'm barely forty," Connelly said argumentatively.

Magoffin was fingering a plug of tobacco. "That's too old for a trading expedition through unknown country—and you and I have been sleeping on Anglo mattresses too long."

Connelly looked again at Ross, then suddenly arose and held out his hand with a smile. "Welcome to Chihuahua, Phillips. Been in Mexico before?"

Ross shook hands. "All my life—off and on."

"Trail experience?"

"Three or four years on the Santa Fe," Ross said.

"I never ran into you," Magoffin said, and it was not an idle remark.

"I think of no good reason why you should have, sir." Ross looked into the penetrating eyes. "I know *your* name, though."

"At that," Magoffin went on thoughtfully, "the cut of your jib has a familiar look."

"You may place it later," Ross said quietly.

"What did you do on the Trail?"

"Everything—teamster, scout, bullwhacker."

"Why?" asked Connelly.

"I liked it. Open country, fresh air, adventure—what more does a man need?"

"Money," said Connelly quickly.

Ross sighed. "I found that out. I put my money into a cargo from China. I thought I was going to make a fortune—but the ship sank in a typhoon near the Philippine Islands."

"How long ago was this?" asked Magoffin.

"The news came in from Guaymas thirty days ago."

"Then you're broke?" asked Magoffin.

"As a businessman, yes. I have some reserve, of course, so I am not compelled to make any deal you offer."

There was silence for a moment. Connelly cleared his throat. Don Fidel reached abruptly for the brandy. The two younger men studied their glasses.

"I didn't mean to pry," said Magoffin.

"You had a right," said Ross. "I want to be under no misrepresentations to you. But I know what my services are worth on this expedition, and if I can't make a profitable deal with you I'll get a job skinning mules for the British running out of Matamoros."

Magoffin muttered, "You're an independent cuss for a man without money." He went on, "I'll be honest. A man who has been unable to make any money on his own is not too appealing to me."

Ross did not answer.

"Had any experience with Indians?" asked Connelly.

"Took my first scalp in the Apishapa—a Ropihue, Old Bill Williams said."

"You knew Bill Williams?" It was a quick question.

Ross shook his head. "*Nobody* knew him. It happened I was trapping castor in the Shining Mountains that summer, and my two partners got done in by redskins crazy for hair. I lit out for the Napestle, and rode into the valley of the Apishapa with four Injuns at my heels. Ran right over Bill Williams' fire, and he cursed me for two days for leading them to him."

"And you got one?" Connelly asked presently.

Ross took the brandy offered by Peralta and tossed it off. "Four. Matter of honor. They made me lose two bales of beaver plews."

Magoffin's keen eyes were on him. "What did Old Bill say?"

Ross looked at the floor for a moment. "It was my first scalp. Old Bill looked them all over and said, '*Sacré, enfant,* must be a God-damned dull knife you sawed them off with!' "

Magoffin roared and hit the table with a huge hand. "He was with Bill, all right!"

Connelly nodded. "He talks like a mountain man when he wipes off that veneer, right enough. Sit down, everybody." He poured another brandy. "The story isn't

38

long but it's damned important." He looked at Ross. "You know that most of the goods that reaches northern Mexico comes by way of St. Louis and Santa Fe or from England through Guaymas. Either way is expensive."

"We sell the stuff and we get our price," Magoffin said, "but we have a lot of competition—Adolf Speyer, José Cordero, John Kelly, Olivarez, Solomon, Macmanus, Anderson—a dozen others."

"It's a long haul," Connelly said. "Nearly two thousand miles, and dangerous every foot of the way: Indians, cyclones, cloudbursts, desert, outlaws—everything in the book."

"Even taking the gold and silver out is risky," said Magoffin. "Since the government prohibits the export of precious metals without a permit—and such a permit would cost more than the metal—then the specie or bullion we take to pay for goods is all contraband and subject to confiscation by Mexican officials. It is getting so it takes a pretty penny in bribery to get the stuff out of Mexico, and now there are so many on the Trail the prices we get for goods drop every season. The risks being what they are, we've had to devise a way to cut the costs."

"In other words, a shorter haul," said Ross.

Connelly unrolled a large sheet of heavy paper with wavy edges. "See here?"

Ross stood up beside him. Ross, taller and more slender, had no trouble seeing, over Connelly's muscular arm, a printed and tinted map of Louisiana and Texas.

"Only about a fourth of Texas has been explored," said Connelly. "The northwest frontier is on a line running from Austin to San Antonio. The rest"—he swept the north and west portions of the area with a quick movement of his thick arm—"unexplored. Inhabited by Kiowas and Comanches. Water is scarce or not fit to drink."

"So I've heard," murmured Ross.

"Ever been in that country?" asked Magoffin.

"No."

Connelly went on. "Precipitous ranges, fast and deep rivers, swamps and bogs, mosquitoes and flies, and the Cross Timbers, which is said to be impenetrable."

Ross, having seen the map, settled down in his chair with a glass of brandy. "You don't think it will be easy."

Connelly seemed slightly disgusted. "I *know* it won't be easy."

Ross looked at him. "I understood that before I came to Chihuahua. If it were easy, you'd send someone of your own."

"Very good," said Magoffin, nodding approval.

"It is not commonly realized," said Connelly, "but Presidio del Norte is a legal port of entry. It was made so four years ago, just before the Texas revolution, but for obvious reasons it never has been used as such. All goods for Chihuahua come through Mexico City on the south, Guaymas on the Pacific coast, Taos in the north, or Matamoros on the east coast. Matamoros is an important point, but it's twelve hundred miles from Chihuahua across the Bolsón de Mapimí, and might as well be in another world. The key to this entire project is the fact that goods can legally enter through Presidio del Norte. Since it is a very tiny post and the commander is of no higher rank than lieutenant, he will be agreeable to whatever the governor suggests. Thus we can get a customs certificate for our goods, and once we have accomplished a legal entry we can take the stuff anywhere in Mexico."

Peralta poured more brandy. The two young Mexicans, Apolinar and Hermenijido, sat stiffly against the wall, eyes wide.

Connelly sat down and fixed his droopy-lidded eyes on Ross. "From St. Louis it is two thousand expensive miles; from Jonesboro or Pecan Point or whatever port we can reach on the Red River of Natchitoches—somewhere in Arkansas or Louisiana—"

Peralta said, "I thought the Great Raft—"

Ross looked up. "The raft was cleaned out of the river last year. The Red is navigable from New Orleans all the way to Fort Towson."

Connelly looked at him. "You probably know all I am going to say—but I want us to be thoroughly in agreement. The expensive part of any trip to Chihuahua is cross-country by ox teams or mules. That part would be shortened to thirteen hundred miles by this proposed route." He paused. "It would give us an edge on competition for a couple of years."

Ross nodded.

"You know this will be a dangerous trip?"

Ross said levelly, "Any time you take a large expedition through Indian wilderness, it is dangerous."

"Knowing that, why did you come on?"

Ross looked at his brandy. "Two reasons," he said, and glanced at Connelly. "First, I found out I was not a trader by sea. Second, putting trading expeditions through the wilderness is my business."

"You think you can recoup your losses on this trip?" asked Magoffin.

"With reasonable luck."

"What if you fail?" asked Connelly.

Ross said quietly: "I've been at this business for ten years and I've never lost a train. I've lost a few men, a few animals, a wagonload of goods occasionally, but never a whole train. That's my business: to conduct pack mules and wagon trains with a minimum of loss. It is also my business to blaze new routes, to find short cuts. I have made my best money that way."

Magoffin said thoughtfully, "It's as good an answer as I could make."

But Connelly had more on his mind. "You will have opposition on many levels. We think Cordero has hired Mangum to stop you. Mangum will hire somebody else to do the job without risking his own neck, and Cordero may hire still another to work independently of Mangum. The man who conducts this first expedition to the Red will have to fight on all these levels."

Ross asked, "And Cordero, too?"

"If you ever work up to Cordero, he will concede. That's the way it is done here."

"Now that you have lost one fortune in a typhoon, what will you do with your share of the profit on this trip?" asked Magoffin.

"Perhaps I would buy a ranch near Chihuahua."

"Why would a man want a ranch in this dry country?" asked Connelly.

Magoffin shrugged. "Some men like champagne—others drink tequila."

Peralta broke in. "You haven't told me, Don Enrique, how you interested the Merchants' Bank of New Orleans in this project."

Ross looked up sharply. "Did you say Merchants' Bank?"

Connelly took it up fast. "Do you know somebody there?"

Ross shrugged. "I know the bank."

Connelly said to Peralta, "Gold and silver bullion from here clears 10½ per cent over gold and silver coin of the United States."

"It's illegal to ship bullion without a license."

"It's illegal to raise tobacco in Chihuahua too," Connelly said, "but I saw a patch of young plants along the road."

Peralta raised his eyebrows, twisted one end of his mustache, and returned to his brandy. "I'm no businessman," he said. "I'm a rancher."

Magoffin said, "You picked up the Merchants' Bank pretty fast, Mr. Phillips."

Ross looked up. "My father is interested in it."

"In what way?" asked Connelly.

"He owns it," said Ross.

Connelly raised his eyebrows. "Then why are you out risking your neck on the trails?"

Ross smiled. "Can you imagine me wearing striped pants and a frock coat, pacing back and forth behind a desk and saying, 'Perkins, write those idiots in Chihuahua and tell them if they get their bullion to New Orleans we'll pay the market price'?"

Magoffin hit the table with a big fist. "He's not a desk man, Connelly. That's obvious!"

"When do you expect to start?" asked Ross.

"Within two weeks—about the first of April."

Ross asked, "What is the Republic of Texas going to say to this?"

"We don't look for trouble. Houston and Lamar are fighting each other, but they both know the establishment of this trade route would be a great thing for Texas. Anyway, we're keeping in the wilderness areas and not going through any settled portion of the republic. We're going to stay north and west of San Antonio and Austin and even Nacogdoches. We'll hit the Red and follow down to Arkansas."

"A lot of unexplored country in there," Ross suggested.

"As far as white men are concerned—yes."

"It ought to be interesting. How about the United States?"

"No trouble there. The merchants favor it; the government encourages it."

"There remains," Peralta noted, "the slight problem of getting bullion out of Mexico and getting goods back in without paying exorbitant duties."

Connelly said with assurance: "Our friendship with Governor Irigoyen will ease the way. He has promised to halve the import duties at Presidio del Norte so as to encourage the building up of trade. It's a good thing for

Chihuahua, since this would naturally be the wholesale center for northern and western Mexico."

Ross set down his glass. "Will we get an open fight out of anybody besides Cordero?"

"Probably not. The stakes are high, but most of these men are in a position to turn their eyes east if the profit lies there. Kelly will watch us carefully. Olivarez will follow Kelly. Adolf Speyer is a man well able to take care of himself; besides, he is backed by Armijo in Santa Fe. Mangum is the man to watch, for I suspect that he has money of his own on the Trail."

"That was his train pulled in yesterday from San Juan," said Peralta, looking up.

"A rough crew they had," said Magoffin. "They spent today sobering up."

"So I heard," said Ross.

"Wagon foreman name of Link Habersham. Know him?"

Ross looked up. "I know him."

"A one-eyed man," said Magoffin.

Ross nodded.

"Had a run-in with him?" asked Connelly.

"A slight one."

"Maybe," said Magoffin, "he'll be your first level to clear out."

"Perhaps," said Peralta, "you'd better not go into town tonight."

Apolinar said quickly, "The Yanqui freighters never bother the *bailes,* Papá. The *fandangos*—yes, of course, but not the *bailes.*"

Ross looked at them both absently. "If there is to be

a fight, let's get it over with. Besides—you have forgotten—I have a duel to take care of in the morning. If there is anything unscheduled, we'd better handle it tonight."

"A duel!" said Connelly. "You're not serious."

Hermenijildo said stiffly, "I am his second."

Magoffin's eyes narrowed. "Who's your opponent?"

"Mangum."

Magoffin shook his head. "This could lead to international complications. He's a British subject. He took out citizenship to get the protection of a British passport."

Ross said indifferently, "Perhaps he will have it with him tomorrow morning."

Connelly was on his feet. "You can't fight a duel. It would cancel the whole project if you were killed."

Ross looked at him and reached for the brandy glass. Peralta sank back with contentment on his face and in every line of his body. "If you ask me, *señores,* I would say Don Felip is looking forward to this duel with pleasurable anticipation. And I will admit that I plan to be there myself. But what an unholy hour to get up!"

"Papá," said Apolinar, "you don't know when the time will be."

"Oh, yes," Peralta grumbled. "Anyone as deadly serious as Mangum could not possibly choose any time but sunrise."

Chapter 3

Ross got up, stretching. "You gentlemen will want to talk it over. Meantime, we'll get dressed for the *baile*."

He led the way to his room. Apolinar left them and went to his own. He was just pushing the door when it opened and a Mexican girl gasped: "¡Oh, *señores!* I am sorry. I was just leaving Don Ross's clean shirt for the *baile*."

"All right," said Ross. "*Gracias*."

He found the white shirt laid out on the bed, beautifully laundered. "Nice-looking girl," he observed.

"Anita?" said Hermenijildo, taking off his jacket. "She's a beauty. Already she has three children and no husband."

"Who's the father?"

Hermenijildo shrugged. "Nobody knows—least of all Anita. She's pleasant, a good servant—but she'd sleep with the devil himself for a silver peso."

"Maybe she has to have a man."

"It's more than that." Hermenijildo frowned. "She gives one the feeling that she is completely without awareness of any principles whatever."

Ross shrugged. "Perhaps that is why the Lord made so many girls—so a man could choose."

Hermenijildo stopped to look at him. "*Señor,* there is one thing I should say."

"Say it."

"Your business is your own, but as your second I

may have the temerity to advise you."

Ross poured warm water out of the crockery pitcher into the heavy basin. "Go ahead."

"I observed your fencing with the men tonight over the reason for wanting to buy a ranch near Chihuahua."

Ross stopped in the course of plunging his hands into the water. "I was not aware I said exactly that—but go ahead."

"I have been with you on three occasions now," said Hermenijildo seriously. "Once at Jennison's *baile* night before last, at the *corrida* today, and again coming home this evening—and on all occasions, *señor,* I observed your conduct in the presence of Doña Valeria."

Ross paused, then plunged his face into the warm water.

"I recall," said Hermenijildo, "that Doña Valeria was visiting in Durango a month or so ago."

"Coincidence," said Ross, wiping water from his face with his hands.

"And you asked us this morning to take you by her house."

Ross grunted.

"You wish to have a ranch near Chihuahua," Hermenijildo said inexorably, "and it is very easy to understand why: because you, being an honorable man, would not ask the hand of Doña Valeria unless you had some goods of your own to offer."

To avoid answering, Ross plunged his face into the water again. Finally he lifted it and said, "You're a romanticist in the largest sense, Hermenijildo."

"I am not old, *señor.* I—"

"Age has nothing to do with it." Ross reached for a linen towel.

"Then perhaps you will leave me a message to be delivered to her in case of your—after the duel tomorrow morning."

Ross chuckled. "If I'm dead, it won't do much good. If I'm alive, I'll deliver it myself. Now, then!"

"*¿Señor?*"

"I don't mind your noticing things, and I don't mind your saying them to me—but no further."

Hermenijildo bowed. "*Sí, señor;* it shall be as you wish."

They left for town about nine o'clock that night, and on the way Connelly and Magoffin began to talk terms, apparently having got over their misgiving caused by Ross's comparative poverty.

Ross agreed on a cash fee of $10,000 and a split of 20 per cent of the net profit for his own work in taking the contraband bullion through the wilderness of Texas and bringing back the goods. Connelly and Magoffin, along with some other American traders and a number of Mexican merchants, would pool their resources and make up a train of some $300,000. This huge sum should be at least doubled on the expedition's return.

Ross said, "This is a fair deal for me except for one thing."

Connelly's question was quick: "What's that?"

"My real profit on this trip lies in the goods."

"You don't call $10,000 a profit?" demanded Connelly.

"No, I don't. That's a fee."

"What do you want?"

"My real profit lies in the goods—and that's something over which I have no control. Through manipulation by government officials the value of the goods can be decreased to nothing."

"You questioning our sincerity?" asked Connelly.

"No." Ross looked at him. "But I know what can happen to the value of goods if the Mexican government becomes unfriendly."

"What's your proposition?" asked Magoffin.

"If my 20 per cent does not equal my cash fee, then I am to get the mules and wagons left at the end of the trip."

Connelly grunted as if he had been hit. "You're asking us to give you $70,000!"

"My expectancy from the net profit is almost that— if not more."

"You're driving a hard bargain. You want to be protected no matter what happens to us."

"This is only in case I deliver the goods as contemplated."

Magoffin groaned. "It's obvious his father is a banker."

"All right, I'll go further with you," said Ross. "If I lose as much on the mules and wagons as 20 per cent of the net profit, then I will forego my claim except for the cash fee."

Connelly said, "Jesús María! What a bargainer!"

"It gives him something to work for," Magoffin noted.

"It puts you in the way of making a fortune," said Connelly.

"The same as you," said Ross. "Likewise, it protects you from loss of your animals. A couple of months' delay and a good norther, and I could be wiped out."

"I don't think our partners will agree to it," said Connelly.

Ross played his trump card. He said quietly: "I have been aware of the clamor in Texas for a short cut like this for at least a couple of years. It is possible I could go there and raise the money to finance an expedition."

Magoffin snorted. "There's not $300,000 cash in all of Texas."

Ross reminded them, "There is still the bank." That was strictly bluff, for his father never had approved of such visionary schemes, and he held his breath for their answer.

Connelly said sourly, "The first venture must succeed if we are to make money—and for that purpose we want the best man we can get." He added, "I'll see what my colleagues say."

Ross suppressed his feeling of triumph.

Magoffin was dubious about one man in the chain: General Conde. "I don't know how he will feel toward this project," he said. "He might have some money in the St. Louis trade, or he might sincerely oppose the contrabanding of bullion. Whatever stand he takes, he will wield a strong influence."

"Can't he be reasoned with?" asked Ross.

"It is difficult. He and Irigoyen often do not see eye to eye. There lies the risk."

"Irigoyen will be governor long enough for us to return."

Magoffin idly slapped his mule's withers with the ends of the reins. "You might be delayed, and Irigoyen might die." He shrugged in the starlight. "A thousand things might happen, but we can only speculate, just as we speculated when we first went to Santa Fe."

The *baile* was at the Cordero house, not far from the plaza. They rode in through the ornate portal, illuminated by smoking wicks in bear oil, and turned their horses over to uniformed servants. The house was similar to Peralta's, as were all Mexican homes when the owners could afford them.

Magoffin and Connelly followed Peralta off to the dining room, where the older men would talk business, while Ross followed Apolinar to the dance, which was held in a large, high-ceilinged room with a rug laid on a dirt floor. The orchestra was a violin, a guitar, and a bass viol, played by swarthy Mexicans dressed in black pants, red sashes, and white silk shirts with wide, flowing sleeves. They played and sang plaintive songs about love and death and disappointment.

There were twenty-five or so ladies in the room, all well dressed in silk and lace, and all black-haired but one—Valeria Sierra. Ross touched Hermenijildo's arm. "She is here!" he said.

Hermenijildo sighed. "I do not have to look, *señor.*"

Ross went to her immediately, and she studied him over her fan. She let him touch her fingers. "I understand," she said, her head tilted a little to one side and her dark eyes filled with humor, "That in New Orleans they have a curious custom of fighting with hats."

Ross bowed. "*Señorita,* New Orleans is a town of many curious customs, but of one thing it has never been accused: failure to appreciate the loveliness of an exquisite lady."

She smiled. "For a Yanqui you are very well mannered."

"I talk better when I am moving," he said. "Will your *dueña* mind if we dance?"

She glanced to one side, where a chunky little brown-skinned woman, sitting in one of the few chairs in the room—a massive thing made of cottonwood—was nodding.

"Probably not, since she is asleep," said Valeria.

The next tune was the Spanish version of a waltz, and the couples began gliding over the rug, the lace mantillas of the ladies floating and swaying gracefully. Valeria raised her arms, and Ross moved in closer and put his left hand, fingers widespread, against her side. She did not wear a corset—few Spanish ladies did— and he realized she had no need for one. They moved out on the floor, maintaining a discreet six inches between them. "*Señorita,*" he said after a moment, "I cannot remember when I have felt such lovely ribs."

There was a smile in her eyes. "The Chihuahuans talk of the moon and the stars. You speak of ribs as if you were buying a haunch of mutton."

He looked down at her. "It is not quite that simple," he said without embarrassment, "nor did I make any reference to sheep. My theory is that you can tell a great deal about a girl by the way she feels when she dances. Some girls are stiff and unyielding; one might as well dance with the statue of Hidalgo."

She danced very lightly, and now she was resting her right arm on his left, and watching him over the edge of her fan. She smiled. "You are married, no doubt, and have many *niños*."

He laughed. "A woman is always direct when it comes to that subject." He looked at her gravely. "As a matter of fact, *señorita*—no. Not yet. However," he said, still looking into her eyes, "in Durango this past winter I saw a girl who changed all my ideas on marriage, and upon my return from Arkansas I hope I shall be in position to discuss the matter with her."

She did not move her eyes from his. "How long will that be, *señor?*"

"Ninety days—a little more, perhaps a little less. Too long, in any case."

When the music stopped, he sensed that something was wrong. He glanced at the wall and saw the girls with their various *dueñas*—mostly short, fat and elderly. He saw the young bloods in a group, handsome with their brown skins and white teeth, beautifully dressed. But they were not talking and laughing together. Without a single exception they faced the door that opened on the courtyard. Hermenijildo stood apart, his eyes unchanged, and with only that gravity of demeanor that since this afternoon had overshadowed everything else. Apolinar stood rigid, his face a little pale.

Ross swung, putting the girl behind him, and faced

the entrance. A big man stood inside the door. The crown of his limp-brimmed hat was even with the top of the doorframe. His red flannel shirt was greasy and torn; his buckskin pants, hardly big enough to hold him, were laced at the front with a buckskin thong; his knee-high boots were wrinkled, worn, and dusty. His face was covered with an untrimmed red beard, and he wore a dirty buckskin patch over one eye.

Apolinar stepped forward quickly, but Ross was in front of him more quickly. "No," he said. "This is my affair." As he faced the big man, he said, "This is a private dance."

Link Habersham fixed his one eye on Ross. "They told me I'd find you here."

Ross took a step forward. "This is no *fandango,* Habersham. This is a private home."

Habersham grinned. "Fancy clothes you got on. Fancier than what you had the last time I seen you, up at Bent's Fort." He turned to the four rough-looking men behind him. They had come inside and ranged themselves in a line. "You like that fufarraw, gents?"

"I like it," said a small fat man whose boot loops seemed too big for him. "That fancy ruffled shirt really shines."

Ross, watching the gleam in Habersham's eye, warned, "You remember what happened the last time you tried to rawhide me—when we were crossing the Cimarron desert."

Habersham didn't grin. "It won't happen this time— no matter how many friends you got here."

Ross saw the girls and their *dueñas* crowding

together at one side; he was aware of their sparkling eyes and held breaths; they loved violence as much as the men. On the other side, the young men were moving restlessly, but Ross held up a warning hand.

Habersham grinned. "I'm gonna pluck out one of your eyes and feed it to the crows."

A whisper came from behind Ross. "This is a matter for the *alcalde*."

"The *alcalde* isn't here," said Ross, keeping his eyes on Habersham. A fourteen-inch bowie knife stuck out of the bullwhacker's waistband. "Give me a knife," he said, holding one hand behind him.

He felt the haft of a knife pressed into his hand, but he did not look around. Bringing his arm to the front, he knew the blade was small and light but he liked the balance of it, and it could be taken for granted it was good Toledo steel.

"Tell your friends," said Ross tightly, "to keep out, or they'll be mowed down with balls." That was strictly a bluff, but he thought it might keep the freighters at bay long enough for him to take care of Habersham and thus avoid a general fight.

They began to circle each other warily, Habersham bent-kneed, not too sure now of his procedure. He was sober, and that in itself was unusual. The man should have been roaring drunk. Therefore this invasion of privacy was premeditated; most likely Link had been well paid. This, then, was the first level on which Ross had to contend. They were wasting no time.

One thing about it puzzled Ross. Mangum not only wanted to block the Arkansas expedition; he also had an intense desire to establish himself as a gentleman. Why wasn't he content merely to go through with the duel? The circumstances argued that Cordero, not interested in Mangum's personal ambition, was intent on confronting Ross with every possible obstacle, feeling reasonably sure that Phillips would not surmount them all.

The sound of Habersham's boots as he circled, the tense breathing of the young men behind Ross, and the sputtering of a candle in a draft were for a moment the only sounds.

Ross moved toward a corner to avoid presenting his back to Habersham's friends. He saw the gleam grow in Habersham's eye, and knew that his opponent anticipated penning him in a corner.

Habersham's eye left Ross's only once—to glance at the tiny knife; then Link, with a sardonic grin, drew the bowie knife with his right hand. A gasp went up from one of the *dueñas* as the huge blade gleamed in the candlelight. Habersham held it wide, moving his hand in a small circle, swinging his arm a few inches back and forth to loosen up the muscles. They were about six feet apart, and Ross, close enough to the walls for protection but not too close to imperil freedom of movement, stopped and waited, balancing on the balls of his feet, and moving a little to keep facing the bullwhacker.

The four men at the door spread out. They were products of the Trail—one of the longest, most difficult, and most violent in history. A man with years behind him on the Trail had not survived by his wits alone. These men were accustomed to violence and to death fights; they expected them and were ready for them.

One thing was in Ross's favor: he, too, had spent years on the Trail—and it never had been easy, for men like Habersham always had distrusted and disliked his manners and speech, learned in a private school. On the Trail, what a man distrusted he sooner or later tried to destroy. Past Habersham's shoulder Ross saw that Valeria's *dueña* was standing on the chair, her eyes wide in her round face.

Habersham lunged.

Ross moved aside, and the big blade went past him. Link moved with such force that it seemed he would bury the knife in the *yeso*-whitened wall. Ross turned in his tracks and made a quick, hard cut with his small dagger in the direction of the man's kidneys. He drew blood, and he knew from the drag on the blade that he had laid open at least half an inch of flesh but the big man had not thrown himself completely into the thrust, for at the bite of the steel he twisted, using the bowie knife like an ax, slashing and hacking.

Ross stepped back, weaving to keep away from the blade. He felt the point bite through the top of his forearm, and leaped to his right to get Habersham off balance. Habersham growled, then lunged again, but this time more cautiously. Ross moved aside. He had taught Habersham respect for the small blade, and now he could afford to wait him out. In that kind of contest he would win, for Link wasn't particularly adept with the knife. He was big and strong, and his bull-like rushes usually won for him. But for work with the blade—

Habersham fooled Ross by leaving his side unguarded for a moment, and Ross stabbed at it with a sidewise cutting action to do the greatest possible damage. But Habersham had known what he was doing. He moved as Ross lunged, and Ross, so sure of his target, could not regain his balance. He tripped over Habersham's out-thrust leg and sprawled on the dirt floor. He rolled instantly, and Habersham's big boots landed where the small of his back had been.

Ross was close to the four men spread out inside the door. He rolled back as Habersham swung a big booted foot at his throat, receiving the blow on the shoulder, but that was better than on the Adam's apple. He sliced the dagger down the calf of Habersham's extended leg and leaped to his feet.

Habersham roared, then whirled as Ross kicked him behind one knee. As Link went halfway down, Ross leaped behind him and slashed. The Toledo steel glittered in the candlelight as it descended a fraction of an inch from Habersham's head and neatly severed his ear. As the grisly object fell to the floor, a sharp intake of breath was heard—from men and women both—that was animal-like in its intensity. Habersham, spread-legged, shook his head in rage. As he turned to face Ross, blood poured from the wound. Nothing but unconsciousness or death would stop him now.

Ross caught movement. The men at the door were starting to close in with murder in their faces. It was time to change tactics. A three-inch dagger against a fourteen-inch bowie knife was good for just so long. He snatched a lighted candle, threw it in Habersham's face, then leaped toward Valeria's *dueña*. The women scattered like chickens before a weasel. He grabbed the chair and raised it above his head, his attackers momentarily pausing as he brought the heavy chair down on the floor and smashed it. He snatched a leg and brandished it before him, then jerked off a table runner of heavy velvet, upsetting three more candles, and wound it, around his left forearm by swinging his arm in a circular motion while he kept the five men at a distance with the chair leg. He held the padded forearm before him and began to advance. The chair leg crunched against a skull, which caved in like a ripe pumpkin.

Now there was activity behind him. The young Mexicans were getting the idea. The four remaining freighters saw that too, and started to rush him, but Ross swung the chair leg viciously. He smashed Habersham's right hand, heard the man grunt, and saw the knife drop to the floor from paralyzed fingers. Then Apolinar and Hermenijildo were beside him, driving the attackers back. The four men broke and fled. One man lay sprawled on his side on the floor, without motion.

Ross heard the dogs bark as the freighters ran through the yard. The girls and the *dueñas* fluttered back into the room and picked up the candles. One stooped by the man on the floor. Ross looked at the pool of blood. "He's dead," he said, tossing away the chair leg and taking a deep breath. "Haul him out." He picked up Habersham's knife, wiped the blade with the velvet runner, and slipped it under his wide belt.

"A very good fight," said a resonant voice.

Ross turned to see Wiley Magoffin standing in the doorway.

Don José Cordero appeared with glasses and a bottle of brandy. He was a tall man, very thin, with a black imperial. "Gentlemen!" he said. "If you will all come this way." He glanced at Ross. "I'm sure the Anglo feels the need of refreshment."

Ross heard an odd intonation in the word "Anglo" and wondered what it meant.

They went into the living room. Cordero, wearing a black waistcoat embroidered in gold, poured brandy for all and offered one to Ross. "*¡Salud, señor!*" Cordero went on: "A very interesting fight. I have not seen that trick of the chair leg before. There's a little too much—brutality about it for our countrymen, I'm afraid."

"I learned it from a master," said Ross, and bowed to Magoffin. "He and I and two other freighters stood together at a *fandango* in Sante Fe."

Magoffin slapped the table. "That's right! That's where it was. And you said you'd never run into me!"

Ross smiled. "*You* said that. *I* said nothing."

Magoffin compressed his lips with pleasure, his eyes alight.

"I remember that fight," said Connelly. "It was the first time I ever saw you, Wiley. I had been in Sante Fe for six months and I was watching him from the Mexican side." He looked at Ross. "There was a boy in the fight—not over fifteen. Was that you?"

Ross nodded. "It was as good a time to start as any."

"That was about ten years ago," Connelly said, speculating.

"Well, gentlemen," said Cordero, "it's a reunion, eh? Shall we drink to it?"

They drank. The musicians were tuning up again.

"You still have the dagger in your hand," said Magoffin.

Ross looked down. The handle was of chased gold and inlaid silver, with a ruby on one side and a diamond on the other. "It's a good blade," said Ross. He got up suddenly. "If you will excuse me?" He bowed slightly to Cordero.

Ross went back to the dance. The musicians were playing again, and the floor was filled. Ross looked over their heads.

"May I have the knife now?" asked a soft voice, and Ross turned to look into Valeria's brown eyes.

"*Señorita,*" he said warmly, "the quality of the blade is exceeded only by the great beauty and the gracious thoughtfulness of the owner."

She was not flustered. "It is a historic weapon," she said. "I am satisfied that it has been well used."

He wiped the blade on his coat sleeve, took it by the point, and handed it to her. "My great thanks, *señorita.*"

Valeria was still looking up at Ross, puzzlement in her clear eyes. "I am curious what kind of man it is who would slice off another's ear. It was one of the most savage things I have ever seen."

"He is no different from any other man," he assured her. "When he is with men who slice ears, he slices ears."

Later, when he found an opportunity, he asked Connelly, "Do you really think Cordero was behind this attack on me in his own house?"

Connelly and Magoffin looked at each other. Finally, Magoffin spoke. "Freighting down the Trail is a gamble," he said. "Last fall Cordero sent a mule train of bullion to St. Louis to buy goods and on the way lost half of it to Indians; his wagonmaster ran off with the other half—and there's no insurance on the Trail."

Connelly added: "If he has sent a couple of hundred thousand dollars East, he sure won't want to take a licking on that—which he would do if his man bought goods in St. Louis and freighted them two thousand miles while we make a quick trip to Pecan Point and return with goods to be sold at half his price."

"Thank you. I hope you will excuse me, gentlemen," said Ross. "I have an unfinished dance." He left them and reached Valeria just ahead of four splendidly dressed young Mexicans who were converging on her but who fell back at Ross's approach. He smiled at them, and took her arm.

Chapter 4

Before the dance was over he saw Hermenijildo standing in the inner doorway, looking grave. When the dance was finished, he took Valeria back to her *dueña* and thanked her in his most flowery Spanish. "And I hope this will be only the first of many such occasions," he said.

She looked at him over her fan. "It may be—if you

are in Chihuahua."

"I'm leaving in a few days," he told her, "but I'll be back."

She said slowly, "It is not advisable to wait too long, *señor.*"

He looked at her, and wished he could speak his heart. "You will be as beautiful all your life as you are at this moment, *señorita.* A few weeks longer will only make you more desirable. And I shall be back."

He thought she blushed behind the fan. She nodded slightly, her creamy lace mantilla, suspended from a very high comb in the back of her blond hair, moving only a couple of inches.

He went to Hermenijildo, still standing like a statue in the doorway. "You need a drink, *amigo,*" said Ross. "Follow me."

He found the older men pleasantly settled around a black walnut table with massive carved legs. Cordero was pouring brandy, and looked questioningly at Ross, who nodded.

Cordero observed, "After such an affair, I should think so." He took two glasses from a servant. "I understand it was a tremendous battle. I'm sorry I did not reach the—arena—earlier." Ross stiffened. "However"—Cordero held out one glass—"I hope for better luck next time."

Ross eyed Cordero fully. "The next time," he said, "I may not be so lenient."

There was abrupt silence in the room.

Cordero raised one eyebrow. "Lenient!" he repeated. "I understand you murdered a man just now."

"You misapprehend, Señor Cordero. The man attacked me with a deadly weapon. The killing was in self-defense."

Cordero looked down at his glass. "Well, I presume the *alcalde* will understand."

"If he does not," Ross said hotly, "there will be a revision of the judicial system in Chihuahua."

Cordero raised both eyebrows. "You question the authority of the law, *señor?*"

Ross got control of himself. "I do not question the law; I question your interpretation of it."

Cordero shrugged as if it were a matter of no moment.

Ross placed his glass on the table. "I shall no longer burden your house with my presence, *señor.* You will excuse me."

He stalked out, followed by Hermenijildo, who whispered: "Don Ross, you insult a very powerful man. Don José will some day be governor of Chihuahua."

"He isn't governor now," said Ross. "And he insulted me first."

Andrés Vigil came hurrying after them with a girl. His dark eyes were luminous. "*Señor,* I wish to go on the expedition with you. You are a great fighter, and I would consider it an honor to load your rifle."

Ross was touched, for the sons of wealthy Mexican *rancheros* usually considered anything short of racing and bull-tailing, attending cockfights and *bailes,* as far beneath them. "Very good," he said. "You shall go, but it will not be necessary for you to load my rifle. You will be too busy loading your own." He looked at the young man. Andrés with his brown, almost golden skin and his dark hair and his neat mustache, was truly, as the Mexicans said, pretty. This did not mean feminine, certainly not in the case of Andrés. Ross glanced at the lovely girl around whose waist Andrés arm still lingered, and said: "We'll be a long time on the road. You'd better take care of your social duties now."

Andrés smiled dazzlingly. "*¡Gracias, señor!*"

Ross watched them sweep away, the girl looking up into Andrés face with adoration in her eyes.

"Mexican girls," Ross noted, "are very easy to hold in the arms, aren't they?"

"*¿Señor?*" Hermenijildo sounded puzzled.

"I have observed the same to be true," Ross noted, "of English girls and Dutch girls and Italian girls—to mention some nationalities offhand—and I have no doubt that a more intensive study would reveal that all girls are, primarily, girls."

"*Señor,* I do not think—"

Ross nodded. "It is confusing, *amigo,* is it not? for I am in high dudgeon against Señor Cordero. Very well, let us resume our walk." He turned on his heel. Head high, unsmiling, he led the way out of the courtyard. Out on the street, Ross stopped for a moment "From the sad look on your face," he said, "I assume Ed Mangum's second got in touch with you."

Hermenijildo nodded. "It is so."

"Who is his second?"

"One Captain Esquibel of the Chihuahua Dragoons."

"Do you know him?"

"By reputation," said Hermenijildo.

"I take it his reputation is not flattering."

Hermenijildo considered. "It is said he has a price."

Ross walked on. "You're married, didn't you say?"

"*Sí, señor.*"

"You like your wife?"

Hermenijildo nodded with great assurance. "She is Chonita, sister of Apolinar. We have been married five months."

"Since we don't want to go back to Cordero's, what do we do?"

Hermenijildo led the way through a narrow, dusty lane toward a door that showed yellow light behind its simple dirty pane. "The Nine Cats," said Hermenijildo. "There we may have a glass of refreshing pulque while we compose ourselves for the ordeal ahead."

They stepped inside, and Ross glanced about quickly as the light fell on him. Hermenijildo was his own height but not quite as slender—a magnificent specimen of manhood, and spectacularly dressed according to the fashion, so much so that for a moment Ross wondered if Hermenijildo had not made a mistake in going into such a poor place. But two or three men spoke to him, and a black-haired girl in a short, bare-shouldered dress flew across the room and fastened her arms around his neck. He smiled and disengaged her and said, "Later, Josefina. Much later."

Then all in the tiny smoke-filled room seemingly became aware of Ross's presence behind Hermenijildo, and the careless talk and laughter died away. But Hermenijildo put a hand on Ross's shoulder and shouted,

"*¡Mi amigo!*" and dropped into a rawhide chair.

Ross sat beside him. "My friend, you have an arm like a bull fighter."

Hermenijildo smiled for the first time that night. "We don't spend all our time counting our money," he said.

A fat Mexican bartender with a long black mustache leaned over the home-made table.

"Bring us some of that heavenly pulque," ordered Hermenijildo, and the saloonkeeper waddled away.

Someone began playing a fiddle, and someone else a mouth organ. The smoke swirled around the room like heavy fog, revealed by one tallow candle. The floor was dirt, of course. The saloon's back room, where the proprietor with his wife and dozen or so *niños* lived, was cut off by an ancient buffalo hide that served as a curtain. In the saloon itself were six or eight Mexicans—all poor, by the raggedness of their shirts and pantaloons, and most of them without shoes, but with feet thickly calloused. There were two girls in the room—both young, both attractive. One sat in the corner farthest from the candle, talking across a tiny table to a bare-footed man whose straw hat was pushed back on his head. The girl smoked a brown-paper cigarette, and they leaned over the table until their heads almost touched. The girl was talking animatedly. The one who had thrown her arms around Hermenijildo had gone to sit in the lap of a heavy-shouldered Mexican, who was kissing her passionately.

"That's Plácido!" said Ross.

"Yes, of course. As you see," Hermenijildo said

above the din, "their pleasures are simple. Should they want more?"

"I am not concerned with the simplicity of the pleasures," said Ross, "for they remain the same in any language and any country. I was thinking of the *niños* that rascal has at home, and I was wondering if they are sleeping on empty stomachs tonight."

Hermenijildo watched Plácido as he pulled the girl's blouse from her shoulders. "His mother-in-law is the old *pordiosera*. Can you blame him for leaving at night?"

"He has money tonight for pulque."

"Yes—and at this moment his mother-in-law probably is taking home a man to console Maria while Plácido is here."

Ross sighed. "I cannot solve your problems," he conceded, "but I wonder at them."

Chapter 5

The proprietor waddled through the smoke and set two great green glasses before them with a flourish. Hermenijildo held up the heavy, crudely made glass and said, "It is not Napoleon brandy, but it has its delights. *¡Salud, señor!*"

Ross smiled and lifted his pulque. He had become well enough acquainted with it to be able to get past the taste of it. The effect of pulque was something else again.

"A place like this has its own attractions," said Hermenijildo.

"So I note," said Ross, his eyes on the girl who now held Plácido's neck so tightly he could not disengage her arms. So Plácido abandoned the idea, and wrestled her onto her back across his lap and kissed her with an abandoned fervor that caused Ross to clench his fist. The Mexican put a swarthy hand on the girl's thigh, as she pressed her half-dressed body tighter against him. Then the outer door swung in and a big form filled the opening.

Magoffin stood there peering around the murky half-light of the saloon. Ross lifted a hand, beckoned and Magoffin came across the dirt floor. Plácido and the girl slipped out quickly behind Magoffin before the door closed.

"Thought I'd find you here," Magoffin boomed, sitting on an upturned wine keg, with his back to the couple talking at the table. "Good place to relax—if you can keep Josefina out of your lap." He glanced at the door. "They say she's insatiable." He looked back with a smile. "Hermenijildo should know."

Hermenijildo drew himself up and said, with dignity, "I am a married man, *señor.*"

Magoffin eyed him for a second, then made a slight bow with an amused smile on his face. "Very well, *señor.*" He looked at Ross. "Mangum has become acquainted with her, they say—and to know Josefina is to sleep with her." He turned to the saloonkeeper. "Pulque."

"I assume you were worried about us," said Ross.

"Hardly worried," said Magoffin. "Worried for the

town, perhaps—but mostly annoyed with Cordero, and concerned that you should stay sober in preparation for the duel." He chuckled. "My wife was there and saw the fight, and she was quite taken with you."

"Your wife?"

"You probably didn't notice her in the room. She comes from a good Mexican family near San Antonio."

"Oh."

"By the way, the man you killed has been identified."

"I don't want to sound callous," said Ross, "but I'm not interested in his name."

"You will be interested in knowing where he came from, though."

"Where?"

"Pecan Point, Arkansas. His name is Kerlérec."

Ross frowned. "The town we are so concerned with, and such a man turns up."

"A strange coincidence, perhaps," said Hermenijildo.

Ross looked at him. "In the Indian country we do not believe in coincidences—or trust them."

"You're wise to say that," Magoffin remarked. "I suppose this trip has been talked about for some time."

"Since last fall," said Magoffin.

Ross studied him absently. "Then it almost looks like a deliberate sacrifice."

Magoffin tossed off a long swallow of pulque. "That it does," he said, wiping his lips with a bandanna handkerchief from the pocket of his black broadcloth coat.

"It looks like somebody heard the town of Pecan Point mentioned and went there especially to recruit a resident. If the man was unlucky enough to be killed by the leader of our expedition, there might be a great deal of trouble at the other end of the trip when our train gets there."

"It's pretty farfetched," said Ross.

"The stakes in the Chihuahua trade are high." Magoffin turned as the girl and the man at the table got up abruptly and went out, each with an arm around the other's waist. The fiddle played dolorously, and the man with the mouth organ wiped his instrument across the leg of his pants and refreshed himself with a glass of pulque. "You must realize the feeling in certain circles of Mexico about the Texas Revolution."

"Most of the Mexicans are in favor of it, I thought."

"That may be—but all are afraid of Texas because rulers and priests have combined to convince the people that the Texans are a nation of depraved criminals who breathe fire and bleed sulfuric acid. Not all of the leaders, of course, and not all of the priesthood—but enough of both to make Mexicans of any class, high or low, insecure where Texans are mentioned." Magoffin lifted his second glass of pulque. "Anything that might show the feasibility of the Texas route eventually will ruin the trade from Independence, and it goes without saying that when that time comes Texans will necessarily control the route."

Ross, watching Magoffin, felt something of the great force of this man whose drive and aggressiveness had already made him a legendary figure in Trail trade as far south as Vera Cruz and as far east as Baltimore. Magoffin had mastered many arts: not only that of shoving a wagon train through wild Indian country but also those of Yankee trading and Mexican bribery, and Magoffin alone knew how many more.

Two peons came in with a black-eyed girl between them, and Hermenijildo held up his empty glass. The girl seated herself on the floor, spreading her yellow skirt around her and folding her legs under it, and the two peons sat one on each side. She looked at one, said something, and laughed at his answer. She looked at the second, said the same thing, apparently, and then laughed again, her black eyes flashing.

Hermenijildo's eyes were half closed as he obviously tried to keep his mind on his pulque.

"There is going to be trouble," Hermenijildo muttered, and Ross, seeing the fire in the eyes of the two men, was inclined to agree.

"By the way," said Magoffin, "Mrs. Magoffin has instructed me to deliver a message to you."

"Not, I hope, to write my mother a letter every night."

Magoffin looked puzzled. "Why do you ask that?"

"Because women who are interested in me always, if they are unmarried, inquire about my wife and children, and if they are married they advise me to write to my mother."

Magoffin got up, his eyes on the girl sitting on the floor. "As a matter of fact, we are going to the opera next week, and she said I am to insist that you be our guest."

73

"Opera in Chihuahua?"

"It's a traveling company—English, I think—and they put on a performance called *The Bells of St. Paul's* or some such name as that. Very popular among the Mexicans; needless to say, it will be one of the high social points of the spring season, since few entertainments come to Chihuahua from the outside world. So get your shirt washed out—the way we used to do just outside of Santa Fe when we slicked up our faces, put new poppers on our whips, and reloaded our cargoes in half as many wagons to avoid the duty."

Ross smiled. "Count on me."

Magoffin turned, a huge man in the tiny smoke-filled room. The girl was practically lying in the lap of one of the Mexicans, and the other Mexican said something that Ross did not hear above the fiddle and the mouth organ. When the other answered sharply, the first leaped to his feet. Yellow light gleamed from the blade of a knife held in his right hand.

The second man pushed the girl to one side and bounded up. The music stopped, and the saloonkeeper shouted at them. But the second man lunged; the first man sidestepped and raked the second man across the chest. The second wheeled, with blood already staining the front of his dirty cotton shirt, and sank his knife to the hilt in the other's ribs.

The stabbed man fell like a log; the blade must have touched his heart. The other, whose shirt now was fully red with his own blood, put the knife back inside his belt and looked around. The girl was gone. He looked down at the man on the floor, snorted, and went out, leaving the door open to the cool night breeze.

The saloonkeeper was rolling the man onto his back and screaming orders at the top of his voice. A small, fat Mexican woman appeared from the back, wringing her hands helplessly.

Ross felt the man's pulse for a moment, then shook his head. "He's dead," he said.

Magoffin jerked his head at Ross, and they went outside, followed by Hermenijildo.

"He'll have to appear before the *alcalde* tomorrow," Magoffin said, "but he'll swear it was a fair fight and he'll show the wound across his chest. The *alcalde* will fine him five dollars for disturbing the peace."

"That's enough to keep him in jail for a year," said Ross. "He never saw that much money in his life."

"His *capitán* will pay it. He works for Conde, I think."

They were walking back toward the square. "What happened to the girl?" asked Ross.

"*¡Oh, sí!*" Hermenijildo exclaimed. "She went away with the man who played the mouth organ."

Chapter 6

It was a cold morning in Chihuahua, with the night wind sweeping down through the black canyons of the Sierra Madres. It was hard waking up, even with Apolinar shaking him by the shoulder, but presently Ross grumbled and got up, stood shivering in his shirt for a moment, yawned, and got into his broadcloth pants.

"It feels like winter up here," he complained.

"It will be warm as soon as the sun comes up," Apolinar said cheerfully.

Ross washed in the icy water, then shaved carefully by candlelight.

"I see why poor people never duel." He spoke without turning his head. "You can't fight a proper duel without a fresh shave, and you can't shave without a light."

"*¿Cómo?*" asked Hermenijildo.

"It's nothing," said Ross. "I guess a man is just as dead with a knife in his back."

"*Señor,*" said Hermenijildo, "you must not be morbid about the killing last night."

"I'm not," said Ross. "I'm trying to shock myself into waking up."

Hermenijildo looked concerned. "Perhaps the cold air will freshen you."

There was a faint knock at the door, and Ross pulled it open. "Come—" He stopped.

The girl Anita was there with a wooden pail full of hot water. "If the *señor* will forgive me, I did not see the light until just now."

"It's all right." Ross took the bucket and thanked her. "She goes lingeringly," he told Hermenijildo. "She wonders what a man looks like who is about to die."

"Or she is choosing a father for her next child," said Hermenijildo.

Ross chuckled. "One might do worse." He poured hot water into the basin. "What time is it?"

Hermenijildo shrugged. "I don't know. I think it's the time the sheepherders get up." He yawned. "You didn't stay out as late as you said."

"I changed my mind," said Ross. "I remembered that daylight comes early."

They went to the dining room and found Don Fidel, fully dressed in his formal clothing of the night before, sipping steaming coffee poured from a pot over a fireplace in the corner of the room. He greeted them and poured coffee for all. Ross sipped his gratefully.

Don Fidel looked up. "The confounded dogs yapping again. It must be friends!"

He went into the patio. The servants were up by that time, and Ross heard faint talking through the heavy cottonwood door. Then Don Fidel came back, followed by the neatly mustached Andrés and his father, Don Mauricio, a very short, round little man with black mustache and goatee.

"How did you know about this event?" asked Don Fidel, pouring more coffee.

"It's all over Chihuahua. It's the first real killing duel that I can remember."

"But the time and the place—"

"Captain Esquibel of the Chihuahua Dragoons, who is second for the Yanqui—*perdóneme, Señor* Phillips. It is thus we think of foreigners of Señor Mangum's caliber."

Ross looked up from his coffee. "You don't like him?"

"Who does?" asked Don Mauricio. "He's a coyote trying to be a *toro*—or is he a *toro* trying to be a coyote?

77

It doesn't matter. He ends up being neither, but in the process he has made many persons miserable."

Ross dropped a piece of brown-sugar *piloncillo* into his coffee. Its fragrance began to clear his brain. "Hermenijildo, you got my revolvers as I told you?"

"*Sí, señor*—likewise the powder flask, extra bullets, percussion caps, bullet patches—"

"Then let's be about our work." He tossed off the last of his coffee. "Since I was forced to get up at such an unholy hour, I'd like to make some use of it, and I can think of no better way to spend the time than taking a shot at the man who caused it."

It was still black; the stars were brilliant; a coyote was singing on a hill west of the ranch. The spicy sweet smell of burning juniper enveloped them for a moment and then gave way to the aromatic fragrance of sage, borne down the canyon on the night wind.

Hermenijildo led, as was his right, carrying the six-shooters and equipment and they followed in a scattered group, saying little. Ross listened to the soft clop of unshod horses' hoofs in the dusty trail, the good creak of saddle leather in the early morning. Presently the sky began to lighten a little over the eastern plains, far across the trackless desert of the Bolsón de Mapimí. Ross yawned briefly, then shivered and shook his head against the morning chill.

"How do you feel?" asked Don Fidel.

"Good enough."

"I don't see how you go through Indian country when you wake up so slow."

Ross looked at him from under heavy lids. "I don't

wake up slow in Indian country."

The sky was much lighter when they trotted through the dusty streets of Chihuahua to the old prison and entered a narrow gate at the back.

The hospital courtyard was about sixty feet long— just right for a duel at point-blank walls. Near the center of the outer wall was a huge old pine tree, and under it were a dozen men.

Magoffin strode out to the gate to meet them; Connelly was at his side, stocky, energetic, quick-moving.

They all shook hands silently. The Anglos were dressed in black broadcloth, as formal as if they were going to the opera; the Mexicans were resplendent in black velvet with red, blue, and green silk, and many huge silver *conchas.*

Magoffin introduced a man Ross had not met: Dr. Jennison, tall, spare, florid, director of the mint at Chihuahua.

"He has consented to act as official physician," said Connelly. "At least you'll have medical attention."

"Glad to see an American," said Ross.

"Do my best to patch you up if you get hit," said Jennison.

Hermenijildo walked stiffly toward the group under the tree on the opposite side.

"We've brought the pharmacist, too," said Connelly. "Von Brauch."

Von Brauch was a big, blond German of military bearing. He snapped his heels together and bowed from the waist. "I am at your service in this hour," he declared.

Hermenijildo came back across the open ground followed by a Mexican officer in the red-and-blue uniform of the Chihuahua dragoons. "Capitán Esquibel," Hermenijildo said, and Ross bowed very briefly.

"He would like to see the pistols," said Hermenijildo.

"Why don't you show them to him, then?"

"*Con permiso.*" Hermenijildo somewhat gingerly handed the two six-shooters to Captain Esquibel, whose dark eyes took them in with professional air.

"He may choose, of course," said Ross.

Esquibel tried both weapons in his hand, first for balance, then for sighting.

"He wishes to show them to his principal," said Hermenijildo.

Ross nodded, and watched Hermenijildo and Esquibel walk back across the yard, then turned his attention to Magoffin and Connelly. Magoffin was telling Don Fidel and Don Mauricio of the fight in the Nine Cats.

"Yes," Don Fidel said impatiently. "He was killed by the best knife fighter in Chihuahua—but who got the girl?"

Connelly looked exasperated. "A man dies—and you are interested only in the girl."

"But the girl still lives—and she must have been *muy simpática* to arouse such a fight."

Hermenijildo returned. "*Señor,* the other principal wishes to load his own weapon."

Ross snapped: "Let him do whatever he wants. Just keep one of those six-shooters in your hand. I loaded them both yesterday, and I don't want to do it again."

"*Sí, Señor.*"

Don Mauricio observed: "Hermenijildo is taking his duties very seriously. His father was a great duelist before the revolution."

Presently Hermenijildo came back, followed by Esquibel, and held out one of the six-shooters. "He will use this one, *señor.*"

Ross glanced at it. "Cap it," he said.

Hermenijildo put caps on all six nipples and handed it, butt first, to Ross. Ross fitted the butt into his palm and pointed it upward. He pulled the trigger six times so fast the shots, crashing upon one another, sounded like the distant roll of artillery fire.

"Very good," Connelly said in a loud voice, to overcome their temporary deafness. "All cylinders fired."

"Of course they did." Ross gave the pistol back to Hermenijildo, who gave it to Esquibel.

"Does he wish powder and balls?" asked Ross.

Esquibel shook his head and started back, with a faint spiral of smoke curling from the muzzle of the pistol. Magoffin moved out of the cloud of smoke, and the entire group reformed some ten feet away. Two doves sitting on the wall went, "*Cú, cú, cú,*" and a crow flapped up heavily from the pine tree and called harshly, "*¡Sangre, sangre, sangre!*"

Ross took six caps from a tin box hanging from the powder flask, pinched them a little, and pushed them on the nipples of his six-shooter.

"You're sure he didn't tamper with the loads?" asked Connelly.

"No, *señor*," said Hermenijildo. "I held it in my hand all the time."

Ross looked across at the knot of men under the tree. "No telling what they've done to the one they're using—but that's none of my business." He balanced the six-shooter in his hand. "I'm ready when—"

"*¡Señores!*" A cry rang out through the courtyard.

Don Mauricio looked. "A peon," he said, dismissing the interruption.

"*¡Señores!*" The cry was almost anguished, Ross thought. He looked toward the gate.

A bare-footed, straw-hatted peon ran across the dusty yard. Ross, seeing the black-and-white mustache, said, "Diego!"

"Why do you interrupt?" Don Fidel demanded sternly.

"*Señor*," said Diego, "it is a matter of life and death."

"I know him," said Ross. "He worked for Olivarez. Let him talk."

"*¡Señor!*" Diego pleaded. "You will believe me?"

Ross glanced at the group under the pine tree. They were watching. He said sincerely, "I will believe anything you say, Diego."

"*Señor*." The man was almost wringing his hands. "My wife—Carlota—she has a sister works for Don Fidel."

Peralta nodded, his eyes narrow, watching.

"She has told me the Yanqui *burro* hired someone to injure the pistol so it will not fire. Please believe me, *señor!*"

"Who did the tampering?" demanded Peralta.

"I do not know, *señor*. She would not tell."

"She would not," said Peralta. "These peons can't be forced to talk if they don't want to."

"It's a job," said Connelly, "to throw you off your balance."

Ross looked at Diego. "It is not impossible," he said, "that some servant has been bribed to plug the touch-holes with soap." Abruptly he raised the pistol and pulled the trigger. There was a soft click. Ross snorted. He pulled the trigger five more times and met five misfires. He looked at Don Fidel's ashen face. "It would seem," he said, "that Diego knew what he was talking about."

"*Señor*," said Peralta, speaking with difficulty, "this is an unforgivable disgrace on my house. I can—I shall never get over it."

Ross said calmly, "You'd better keep an eye out for the traitor." He turned to Diego. He started to reach into his pocket, then remembered. He slapped Diego hard on the shoulder. "*Gracias, hombre, mil gracias.*"

Diego beamed with pleasure, and backed away.

"*¡Un momento!*" said Ross.

"*¿Señor?*"

Ross took half a dozen steps toward Diego. "Why did you do this?" he asked. "You knew it might be dangerous to interfere."

Diego shrugged. "One does not refuse to do a thing just because it is dangerous, *señor*—if one knows it is right."

"True enough," said Ross. "If you ever need help, *hombre,* I shall feel hurt if you do not let me know."

Diego smiled and started to leave.

"Don't you want to watch the duel?" asked Ross.

Diego shook his head. "I am sorry, *señor*. We must get an early start this morning across the desert. It is slow with a burro and four children."

Ross nodded. *"Vaya con Diós, hombre."*

He went back to Hermenijildo and held out his hand for the powder flask. "There's a hatpin in there to clean out the holes," he said. "Otherwise we'll be here all day trying to draw the loads."

"Señor," said Peralta, trying to recover his voice, "this is the greatest shame in my life."

Ross felt sorry for him. "We were warned," he said. "No harm has been done."

Ross picked at the holes with the pin while Connelly fumed. "That would have been murder."

Ross held the pistol in the air once more and tried it. Five cylinders fired, again filling the morning air with a crescendo of shattering explosions. He moved out of the smoke cloud and worked once more on the sixth cylinder, finally got it cleared, and fired it. Then he examined all nipples carefully, and called for powder and ball.

He measured the charge of coarse powder, set the ball on a linen swatch, and drove it home with the loading lever. When all were loaded, once again he capped the nipples, pulled the trigger to half-cock, turned the cylinder, and inspected each chamber thoroughly. For the first time, he felt nervous. He had almost walked into a death trap; for the other man, filled with the knowledge that he would not be in the way of hot lead, could have taken his time and made the first shot good. Ross handed the pistol to Hermenijildo.

Heads were looking in at the gate, and Mexicans began to file in to watch this strange satisfaction of honor, as formal to them as a dinner with linen and silver and fine wines.

"Quite a crowd here," observed Dr. Jennison.

Wolfgang von Brauch sized up the street wall. "At least forty witnesses," he noted.

The two groups came together. Von Brauch was to direct the duel. "You will stand back to back in the center. I shall call, 'One, two, one, two,' and you will march forward. When I call 'three, four,' in the same cadence, at the word 'four' you will turn and commence firing. You will continue until your loads are exhausted or one man is down. Is it agreed?"

"Yes," said Ross, for the first time looking at Mangum, and again wondering at the deadly intensity on the man's square face—a hunger, almost.

"Take your places," said von Brauch.

Ross walked to the center of the yard, aware that Mangum was slightly behind him. Hermenijildo handed him his six-shooter, and he glanced to see that all caps were still in place.

Von Brauch said, "I am ready to count. . . . One, two, one, two—"

Ross marched out, listening for the "three, four." The doves had risen from the wall after the last round of shots, but the crow was still swooping and wheeling over the yard and calling its raucous "*¡Sangre!*"

"One, two, one, two—"

Ross was marching toward the east, and the sky was well lighted, although the sun would not be above the wall for some time. He no longer smelled the pungent powder smoke, but was aware of the fragrance of apple blossoms. It was a mild surprise to him, because he had supposed they would bloom much later so high in the mountains.

"One, two, three, four."

His right foot was forward, and he swung to the left.

Mangum fired, and almost immediately was obscured by a cloud of white smoke. Ross fired—more to hide himself than anything, and then waited.

Mangum stood where he was, for Ross could see his feet. A yellow explosion blossomed from within the smoke, and Ross fired at it.

Mangum answered twice before Ross fired again. Mangum fired a fifth time, and now of course they had to judge position entirely by their feet. The shots echoed loud and crashingly from the walls of the prison yard, and Ross thought the rifle shots must have sounded much like that to Hidalgo in the instant before he died.

Mangum fired his sixth shot, and Ross answered.

Mangum stepped from the cloud, and Ross aimed at him deliberately.

Esquibel shouted suddenly, and Mangum for an instant looked blank, then started back into the smoke cloud.

Ross could at least have winged him then, but he held his fire. He had no wish to shoot an unarmed man and certainly none to kill him, even though he disliked him. The shot would have been justified, since Mangum had taken his six shots, but Ross hesitated. Almost immediately he realized that he was in an embarrassing position, for he was still entitled to a shot, and the Mexicans, meticulous in such things, would wonder why he did not use it. As a matter of honor, of course, Mangum should come out of the smoke and demand that Ross take his shot. But Mangum stayed in the slowly thinning cloud while Ross stood, his elbow bent and the pistol pointing at the sky, trying to think of some way out without shooting at the man. Mangum, of course, had already disgraced himself by taking refuge.

While he hesitated, a mounted man galloped through the gate and shouted, "¡Señores! ¡No más! A paper from the governor!"

He rode up to von Brauch and stopped his horse with a great flourish befitting the occasion.

Von Brauch stepped up, took the paper, and glanced through it. Ross stood his ground.

Von Brauch looked up. "Gentlemen! This is an order from Governor Irigoyen prohibiting a duel between any subject of Her Britannic Majesty and a citizen of the United States under pain of a heavy fine and prison sentence." He looked at Ross and then at Mangum, from whom the smoke had arisen to reveal him as a perfect target. "I am forced to say, gentlemen, that this order comes too late. One principal has fired six times, the other five; therefore I take the responsibility of ordering the duel continued until the twelfth shot is fired."

Ross aimed. Mangum was now a clear target, his arms at his sides, the empty six-shooter in one hand. Ross lowered his pistol and said: "Herr von Brauch, it is not my wish to cause you difficulty with the governor. I therefore reserve my shot until the next meeting."

Von Brauch bowed. "As you wish, Herr Phillips." He waved one arm. "Gentlemen, the duel is over. Do the principals wish to shake hands?"

Ross glanced at Mangum. Ross had no great desire to make peace with Mangum, but he did not want to be rude. But Mangum turned his back and stalked away.

Ross's arm dropped. Connelly took the pistol. Magoffin said, "I thought I saw a bullet tick your coat, but there was so much smoke I must have been mistaken."

Connelly had walked around behind Ross, and exclaimed, "It went through his coat!" He stared at Ross. "How did it get there?"

Ross felt his eyelids drooping in spite of himself. The pistol dropped from his fingers. "How the hell do you think?" he asked. "It went through me first!"

Chapter 7

The ball had indeed gone through Ross; but, fortunately, it had not touched any vital organ. The wound was painful, but healed well in the next few days. Dr. Jennison and Dr. Connelly both attended him. Short of infection, there was no danger, though Connelly thought they had better put off the start of the expedition. But Ross was back on his feet within a week, and would not hear of it.

"I'll be able to ride without losing blood," he said, "in another week—and time is important. There will be grass for the animals by April first, and with good luck we can make the trip to Pecan Point, take care of our business in New Orleans, and return to Chihuahua before the northers set in."

Dr. Jennison shook his head, but Magoffin and Connelly had been long on the Trail, and they agreed that if there was no infection the wound was but an incident. Magoffin explained it to Jennison:

"If we stopped for every bullet and arrow wound, it would have taken us ten years to make a round trip."

"Most of the time," said Connelly, "a man is pampered too much when he gets hurt."

Jennison shook his head. "I admit I am but an ordinary frontier practitioner, and most of my practice is limited to those who more or less 'enjoy' a moderate spell of sickness."

Ross was hospitalized in a large bed in a cool room of Connelly's home in Chihuahua. An early visitor was the *alcalde,* a small, very slight Mexican with gray hair and mustache. He came to hold a hearing over the killing of the freighter. Cordero was not present.

The hearing was held in Spanish, with the *alcalde* asking questions. "You knew this man Link Habersham?"

"Yes," said Ross.

"And those with him?"

"One of them."

"You knew the one you killed—Kerlérec?"

"Not at all."

"You did not?" The *alcalde* seemed astonished.

"Never saw him before."

"Then why did you kill him?"

"Because he attacked me with a bowie knife."

"You have the marks?"

Ross bared his forearm, where the welt was eight inches long.

"This was made by the man you killed?"

"No. By Habersham."

"But I do not understand. Why was Habersham fighting?"

"He started it."

"For what reason?"

"I don't know." Ross grinned suddenly. "Maybe because I gouged out his eye up on the Cimarron."

"Is it true that you sliced off his ear?"

Ross nodded. "It is."

"That is a crime also."

"When it's self-defense?"

"But, *señor,* you can hardly plead that slicing off an ear is self-defense."

Ross drew a deep breath and looked at the old man. "*Señor,*" he said solemnly, "picture me fighting a man who is trying to disembowel me with a fourteen-inch knife. He is a man with big ears. Would you consider it wrong for me to slice off an ear in self-defense?"

The old Mexican studied him absently, obviously trying to visualize this situation. "Perhaps not," he said at last. "But there is one more question. You know it is against the law to have a weapon in Chihuahua?"

"Never heard of it."

"I am informed that you attacked these four men with a dagger for which you have no permit."

Ross lowered his eyes significantly. "Have you been told it was a small blade with jewels on it—such as might have belonged to a woman?"

"*Sí.*"

"Then," said Ross, "I can only testify that it is an affair of honor, and I feel sure the gallantry of a Mexican gentleman will not require me to name the lady involved."

The *alcalde's* eyebrows lifted; this, of course, was a new aspect of the matter, and one which he could well understand.

Connelly moved forward and shook hands with the *alcalde,* thanking him for his courtesy and suggesting that the patient was weary and should not be questioned further. The *alcalde* bowed out.

"Well," said Ross, "that was easier than I expected."

"You showed an astonishing understanding of Mexican law and customs," said Magoffin.

Ross chuckled. "The best knowledge was exhibited by Dr. Connelly when he slipped the gold doubloon into the *alcalde's* palm."

Connelly waved it away. "Sixteen dollars well spent. Now! Let's get on with our plans. I've been looking at mules and I've got fifty dragoons promised as a guard."

"Dragoons!"

Connelly chuckled. "If the governor sends them, I don't have to pay them."

"Don Fidel is here," said Connelly.

Ross brightened. "How about the brandy, Doctor?

Don't you have some brandy for special guests?"

"To your health, Señor Phillips," said Don Fidel. *"Gracias."*

"Now, when is this young rooster going to be out?"

"In two days," said Ross.

"Good. You know, of course, he is released on bond?"

Magoffin spluttered. Connelly swore softly.

"Ten thousand dollars," Don Fidel said, licking the brandy from his lips.

"Ten thou—"

Connelly swore softly.

Don Fidel said cheerfully, "The brandy we have received from Paso lately," he said, "is too green."

Ross was walking around in two more days, and two nights later Apolinar brought his best clothes from Los Saucillos and helped him to dress for the opera as solicitously as a valet dressing a matador. The white shirt-front, the flowered brocade waistcoat, and the black broadcloth coat and pants, not to mention the wide, flowing black cravat—all had to be exactly so to Apolinar's eye.

Magoffin came by to get him in a heavy, lumbering carriage pulled by five mules. "It's no better than a farm wagon," Magoffin said, "but it's what the Mexicans like and recognize—and style is important to us here."

Mrs. Magoffin was a very beautiful woman of medium height and typical Spanish coloring.

"I have heard so much of you," she said, with a delightful accent and a lilt in her voice that reminded him of Valeria. And as he thought of it, he realized it had been hardly more than a week since he had seen Valeria, but it seemed like months.

"—an excellent duel," Mrs. Magoffin was saying, "and Enrique says you acquitted yourself extremely well. I am curious about one thing," she said, studying him from the depths of her liquid black eyes. "You had every right to shoot the man, and he's a peeg and everyone knows it, and he had taken six shots at you, and you knew he tried to kill you—why didn't you kill him and get it over with?"

"Gertrude!" said Magoffin in mock horror. "I never knew how bloodthirsty you were."

"Is nothing," she told him. "I am as softhearted as any woman, but I have lived in frontier country all my life, and I have seen men fight, and I know a man may not get a second chance."

Ross drew a deep breath. "For one thing," he said, "we're not on the frontier. For another thing, I'm not afraid to give a man like him a second chance. That will even up the odds."

They entered the opera house by a side door. It resembled a Yankee opera house except that it was smaller and the arrangements were not as luxurious. The stage seemed fairly primitive, but it was raised and had a wooden floor. Boxes were ranged around the room on the second level, and the Magoffins entered one of them and arranged their straightback chairs.

"It's an English company," Magoffin was saying, "and the words are in English, and to save my soul I can't understand what the Mexican people see in it, but it's the most popular opera in Mexico."

Below them, on the main floor, were some simple benches without backs, but these were placed in the rear third of the room. The first two-thirds were the bare dirt floor, and there the peon women sat with their legs folded under their skirts, packed incredibly closely together but taking it all in great good humor, and smoking one cornshuck cigarette after another as if they were afraid to lose the light, and constantly passing a lighted cigarette back and forth to someone else.

"Dr. and Mrs. Jennison have arrived," said Mrs. Magoffin.

She took a cigarette from a pack tied together with string and leaned over as Magoffin held a sulphur match for the light. Magoffin himself worked off a chew and offered one to Ross, who declined.

The space below was filling up, and the boxes all around the room were showing activity.

Then, for an instant, Ross stared. Across the room, directly opposite, the dazzling beauty of Valeria Sierra seemed to light up the entire room.

"She is most lovely," breathed Mrs. Magoffin.

But Ross said nothing, for at her arm was Ed Mangum, arrayed in the most gaudy Mexican costume permissible in such a place. Behind them was the *dueña*, who came in quietly and sat in the rear, while Mangum made a great show of helping Valeria with her black lace mantilla.

Ross got up, his underjaw working. "I'm going out for a drink," he said shortly. "Will you excuse me, *señora?*"

She had followed his eyes, and now she shook her head sympathetically. "I am so sorry," she said. "I did not dream this would happen."

Ross looked at her for a moment, then sat down again. He might as well endure it. But Mrs. Magoffin was right; he should have killed the man while he had a chance.

Chapter 8

The next several days were busy ones. Ross drove himself as much as he dared. With Mangum, the Mexican Yanqui who was neither the one nor the other, courting the Doña Valeria, there must be no mistakes on Ross's part. Stores piled up in Connelly's warehouse; Ross bought mules and seven American wagons from Adolf Speyer, and began to hire men.

This train would be one of the greatest caravans ever seen in northern Mexico—seven hundred mules, no less, for Connelly said they were counting on $300,000, mostly in silver bullion. Nothing else was talked about in the Nine Cats or in the public granary. Arellano's nine swords were forgotten. And not the least element of satisfaction was in the fact that the Chihuahueños had been so long under the rifles and arrows of the Comanches, and that they now felt a symbolic pride in knowing that the caravan would go through the heart of Comanche land.

They hired Plácido as a *mayordomo* for the *arrieros,*

the muleteers. Connelly said he would drive the mules until their shoulder blades stuck through their hides. "He will get more out of the mules and men, and cheat you out of more money for feed when you reach Arkansas, than any *arriero* in Mexico."

"How can he leave Josefina?" asked Ross.

Connelly shrugged his heavy shoulders. "Perhaps you will tell me when you get back." He stared across the plaza. "How is Josefina going to get along without Plácido?"

Don Fidel furnished a beautiful black gelding for Ross to ride on the trip. It was not a typical Spaniard's horse, for it had strong legs and a short barrel, a deep chest and strong neck, wide head and intelligent eyes. As Ross rubbed its muscular withers, the horse's head swung around to inspect him, and Don Fidel said with satisfaction, "A good sign."

Apolinar was going on the trip, Don Fidel said, to learn something besides bullfights and cotillions. And when Hermenijildo came to arrange for the loading of the bullion, he was on horseback, accompanied by his wife and three servants on mules. Hermenijildo was very attentive as he helped her down from her box-like sidesaddle. Chonita, a full head shorter than her husband, had sparkling black eyes and quick movements and an awareness of everything about her.

Ross said, "*Señora*, I have long wanted to meet the wife of the man who assisted me so ably."

She smiled up at him and said simply, "*Gracias.*"

He went on easily: "I had built up quite a picture in my mind of a very beautiful and charming creature who alone would be worthy of the devotion of such a stanch one as Hermenijildo, but now I find I must revise my wondering to speculate on how Hermenijildo could merit the faithfulness and devotion of such an extremely attractive woman as you are."

She smiled as if it was a great secret between them. "And I in turn have wondered, *señor,* what kind of man could be so pretty"—she meant "handsome"—"and at the same time make such lovely speeches."

He raised his eyebrows. "I have been making other such speeches?"

Laugh crinkles formed around her eyes. "You have said to her, 'I cannot remember when I have felt such lovely ribs.' And the *señorita* answered, 'You speak as if you were buying a haunch of mutton.' Shall I go on, *señor?*"

For a moment he was astounded; then he smiled. "Perhaps it will not be necessary, *señora,* for I am sure your husband has heard it many times already." He looked at Hermenijildo, whose face did not change. "Is there nothing sacred in Chihuahua?"

"In a courtship," she told him mysteriously, "many curious things may happen."

"Thank you for warning me."

"But, *señor,* you must not think of that when you are dancing with the *señorita.*"

"This—mind reading—might be useful in other ways," he noted.

"Yes, *señor?*"

"For instance, what does Señor Mangum say to Señorita Sierra?"

97

"Ooh! Very dull things." Her face suddenly became as sober as Hermenijildo's; the twinkle went out of her eyes, and for a moment her face looked very plain.

" '*Señorita,*' " she mimicked, " 'do you think Santa Anna will again be president of Mexico? What is your opinion of the right of Texas to claim her boundary to the Rio Grande? What of the state of trade? Do you not think Mexico's future lies west, toward China?' "

This was so absurdly un-Mexican that Ross could not restrain a smile. "And what did the *señorita* answer?"

Chonita shrugged expressively. "Who needs to answer a man like that? He answers himself."

A servant took away her black horse.

"Then I take it his courtship of her is not very serious."

Her eyes opened wide. "On the contrary, *señor!* It is very serious. For one thing, it is different. For another, no person is as completely ignorant of what she should do as a girl in love."

"In love?"

"But of course, *señor.* All Chihuahua knows that she is in love with you. It is simple, *verdad?*"

"I confess I find it not only not simple but actually not understandable."

"She is much taken with you, *señor,* and you have only to say the word and she is yours. But in the meantime, you do not expect her to sit home and make tortillas while you debate your mind—especially when a man is ardently pursuing her."

Ross drew a deep breath. "I—she—"

"Perhaps you are not a man who wants to marry, *señor.*"

"On the contrary," he said, "I have been thinking about it very seriously for the last several months."

"Then, *señor,* are you afraid to speak—you who are not afraid of bullets?"

"No," he said earnestly. "No, I—you see, *señora,* it is hardly fair that a man setting off on a dangerous mission from which he may not return should—"

"What is to be lost?" she asked.

He floundered. Obviously those who knew he was without funds had kept it to themselves, and he could not under any circumstances reveal it to the woman, for it would be the same as asking Valeria to marry him but confessing his condition. It wasn't that Valeria would be repelled by his poverty, for she had plenty of money, and she was the kind of woman who would share it— but Mexican custom positively would not allow it. There was only one answer: he must have money before he asked her to marry him.

Chonita looked at him wisely. "Don't take too long, *señor.* A girl in love is most vulnerable—not only to the man she loves but to others."

He looked away at the rocky peaks of the Sierra Madres, unknown, unknowable. A woman's ways (beyond temporary love affairs or a flirtation) were like the distant mountains—unknown and unknowable except to other women.

He watched Father Ramón in his garden some distance away while Hermenijildo took Chonita into the house.

Hermenijildo returned. "*Señor,*" he said, looking up and shading his eyes with his hand, "I hope you do not take it amiss that my Chonita has advised you in your relations with Doña Valeria."

"Not at all."

"This is a woman's privilege, *señor.*"

Ross looked down at him. "I have no objection."

"*Gracias*—and now I have a question."

"All right."

"You have not assigned me my post."

"Post? You're busy eighteen hours a day, aren't you?"

"On the expedition, *señor.*"

Ross frowned. "I didn't know you were going."

"But *seguro.*"

"You're just newly married."

"Chonita will wait for me."

"But—"

"*Señor,*" Hermenijildo said earnestly, "I am young and have good health, and this is a project that means much to the entire state of Chihuahua and perhaps to all of northern Mexico. It is not too much that some of us forego the comforts of a warm bed for a little while to help assure the success of an enterprise that means so much to Chihuahua and my people."

"Very well," said Ross, getting down. "You go along as my assistant." He pulled up his belt. To tell the truth, he rather liked the idea, for Hermenijildo was one of the most dependable men he had known. And although he did not say so, he knew there were other factors that impelled Hermenijildo: a love of adventure—for Hermenijildo had been close to home all his life; and, not least by any means, a desire to prove himself in the eyes of his wife.

"Can your grandfather take care of the mine, then?"

"Yes. He is not old—sixty, maybe."

"And he is there by himself?"

"Yes."

"And Chonita will stay at your place?"

"No, it's too isolated. Sometimes the Apaches sneak down from the mountains—and Chonita is *preñada*." He smiled happily.

Ross nodded. "In that case she will want to be with her mother while you are gone."

Ross rode up into the mountains with him, and went down into the mine, where bars of silver, 50 to 80 pounds each, were stacked to the ceiling of a room dug out of the rock. Each bar was stamped with the royal seal and its fineness was marked on it. The room and the mine itself were guarded by two fierce-looking men with rifles.

"How much is in here, Hermenijildo?"

"About 120 *arrobas*."

Ross did some multiplying in his head. "About three thousand pounds," he noted. "That is short of the goal, isn't it?"

"Dr. Jennison at the mint has been buying, and Señor Connelly said yesterday he had enough silver and gold to make up the total."

"We'd better bring enough mules Tuesday morning to haul this stuff into town."

"*Sí, señor.*"

He found Magoffin and Connelly at Los Saucillos when he returned, and they went into a discussion of plans. "We can load 150 pounds to a mule," Connelly said, "so—"

They heard the dogs barking, and Apolinar looked from a tiny window deep-set in the thick adobe walls. "It's Andrés!" he said. "Something must have happened!"

Magoffin and Connelly rushed to the courtyard. Andrés had galloped through the big gate and now dropped his reins and came toward them. He seemed oblivious to all but Ross Phillips. "¡Señor!" he cried. "A very sad thing has happened. My father will not permit me to accompany you on the expedition!"

Ross thought quickly. "Perhaps he needs you at home."

"I do not know. He says that I may not go."

That a well-bred young Mexican should so impulsively report his parental injunction to someone outside the family indicated to Ross how overwhelming was the boy's desire to go and how complete his confidence.

"Perhaps he will change his mind."

"I have hoped, *señor,* that you will speak to him, and show him the importance of this expedition to our country. Perhaps then—"

"Tomorrow night," Ross said, "I'll see him at the governor's reception, and I'll try to broach it to him."

"Thank you, *señor!*"

Don Fidel revealed that he too understood that Andrés was very upset. He said: "You need a glass of brandy, Andrés. The sun is hot, and that bay has a ragged gallop that would jar juice out of a mesquite root."

Andrés began to recover his control. *"Gracias,"* he said with a slight bow.

When he was gone, Magoffin said to Don Fidel: "That's a sample of what you Mexican fathers are doing to your sons. No wonder they don't engage in daring adventures. You won't let them!"

Don Fidel chuckled. "Fortunately, I can overlook that, because Apolinar is going. However, you are right, *señor.* We build up great estates and we have a son and we want him to fill our shoes, and we expect him to do it without training or experience because we are afraid he might get hurt." He lifted his glass. "It is so all over the world, is it not?"

Connelly agreed. "Too bad. Andrés is nearly twenty. When I was twenty I had been on the Trail five years."

Don Fidel sighed. "True—and a lot of others were on the trail with you at that age." He added soberly. "Most of them have been dead a long time."

"Those who are left are good men," said Magoffin.

Connelly looked at Ross. "I'm really most worried about the Comanches. I've been on the Trail for twenty-five years, but I haven't done much freighting in unexplored territory. What's your idea, Ross?"

"The best protection against Indians is other Indians, so I've always found, and this morning I engaged four Tonkawas as spies. The Tonks hate the Comanches anyway."

Magoffin nodded. "That will take care of the

Comanches. *I'm* more worried about the Texans."

Connelly said: "I talked to President Lamar when I was in Austin last winter. Everybody in Texas is as much interested as we are. The only thing is, as far as Texas is concerned, it has to be unofficial to avoid starting a ruckus with the Houston camp. That's why we're skirting the Texas towns and keeping to the wilderness."

Ross put down his glass.

"As soon as you leave," said Connelly, "I am going to New Orleans, and it will be my job to explore all possible avenues of making a profit. It may be that we can persuade the United States Government to allow us a drawback on goods exported to Chihuahua, to get the trade established."

"And," said Magoffin, "you may have to smooth the Mexican consul's sense of duty so he will neglect to report that a merchant from Chihuahua is buying a third of a million dollars' worth of goods—for if news of this gets to Mexico City, there is no telling where it will stop!"

Chapter 9

At Irigoyen's reception the governor had a talk with Ross and suggested he be discreet about the bullion he might be taking. Ross also met General Conde, a large, portly, florid man with a cynical eye who did not like Texas or Texans. Mrs. von Brauch, a small, vivacious French woman, talked delightfully, but Don Mauricio Vigil was unmovable on the subject of Andrés.

Ross could hardly get a chance to talk to Valeria, for Mangum was there, and the Corderos seemed to have taken him under their wing and to be determined to keep him as much as possible with Valeria. He finally conceded to himself that the drawing room was not his forte, and found Magoffin with Connelly and von Brauch and Irigoyen discussing Josiah Gregg and his operations on the Trail, and the great fight at the *fandango* in Sante Fe when Lewis Garrard took part, and the subsequent adoration of the lustrous-eyed Mexican girls, always generous to the conqueror. Ross got a large glass of brandy and sat back against the wall. . . .

On April second he took two hundred mules to the mine to load the silver. Plácido, in all the glory of his ragged pants and bare feet and his undoubted virility, supervised the packing. A mule's eyes were covered with blinders, and a soft sheepskin was thrown over its back as a saddle blanket. Plácido saw to it that all sheepskins were smooth and free of wrinkles. Then a saddlecloth was laid over it, and the packsaddle was put on top of that. The packsaddle in this case was in the nature of a double saddlebag, since silver was very heavy and would not require much space. Plácido also tightened the broad grass saddle-girths, with one knee on the mule's belly to hold it in. A grass packrope was thrown over the whole and then under the mule's belly in some pattern known only to Plácido himself.

All this was done with remarkable swiftness. Plácido, on the mule's near side, finished fastening the last rope and cried, *"Adiós,"* and his assistant, on the other side, sang out *"Vaya."* Plácido tossed the end of the rope over the cargo, cried, *"¡Anda!"* and the mule trotted off to join its companions.

Ross issued strict instructions as to the number of bars to be packed in each packsaddle making sure there would be no more than 150 pounds to the mule—three small bars or two large bars.

The two hundred mules were quartered in and around the plaza that afternoon, under guard of Esquibel's fifty dragoons and watched over by Connelly and Magoffin, who rode herd, assisted by Apolinar and Hermenijildo, all night. All four were mounted, and spent their time riding around the area in opposite directions. The man who had been Mangum's second was trusted by no one.

The next morning at daybreak Ross found Plácido already rousing up the *arrieros* for the trip to Los Saucillos, and by mid-morning five hundred more mules were loaded with a fortune in gold and silver, and Plácido turned them north.

They were joined in Chihuahua by the first two hundred, in single file. It took almost an hour to cross the little bridge over the irrigation ditch on the road out of Chihuahua, for the entire caravan was over two miles long. First went half of the dragoons, then three hundred and fifty mules, then the wagons, then the rest of the mules, and finally the rest of the dragoons. They would have to close up ranks as soon as the mules became trail-broken, for they were too vulnerable to Indian attack—but that would come later.

Half the town of Chihuahua was there to watch them leave. Girls and women waved to men in the train, *arrieros* and soldiers, and these grinned broadly and shouted back, then turned and followed the mules.

Esquibel with thirty dragoons led the way north toward El Paso del Norte. The dragoons were a fierce-looking set of ruffians with swarthy faces and great mustaches. One in particular was a bigger-than-average Mexican with a badly pockmarked face. Ross suspected they were the kind that marched southwest when the Comanches attacked from the northeast. However, once they got the train beyond reach of Chihuahua, and especially after they crossed the Rio Grande, there would be no place for them to retreat, and so it might be expected that they would fight. There was no attempt at uniforms; they wore the usual ragged pants and shirts; high boots when they could find them, and big hats, though they favored felt rather than the straw of the peon, which was a mark of bondage. Their rifles were most indifferent—all muzzle-loaders, most of them flintlocks, a few converted caplocks; and three of them had only bows and arrows.

"It's quite an army," said Connelly with sarcasm in his voice.

"They give us one advantage," Magoffin pointed out. "The Indians are not likely to attack a train with so many men."

The Tonkawa scouts, bareheaded, wore breech-clouts, buckskin shirts, and leggings of deerskin; they rode their wiry mustangs bareback.

Apolinar was nominally in charge of the seven

107

wagons, each of which was pulled by eight mules hitched to a chain. Because the wagons held their food and feed, and extra arms and powder and lead, their position was in the middle of the train.

They had an *arriero* for every eight or nine mules, and this would be sufficient, for on the trail each mule would follow the other's tail once they got the orneriness boiled out of them by the sun.

Ross sat the great black gelding alongside Connelly and Magoffin and Don Fidel; Hermenijildo was at his side. Connelly was nervous. "If anything happens," he said, "there'll be a lot of us broke for a long time to come. That's a whopping big amount of bullion. Most of us have plenty of money in land or animals, but that much in cash is a lot."

"You can be sure of one thing," said Ross. "The Comanches would rather have the mules than the silver."

The long, long train wound up to the pass on the north, where they would go through the mountains, which seemed impenetrable from where they watched. The first detachment of Esquibel's troops were far out of sight.

A slender, bare-legged girl burst shrieking from the crowd that lined the street and ran to throw her arms around an *arriero*. Plácido came by and grinned at them; he was riding a big California mule.

"I wonder where Josefina is," said Connelly.

"Probably looking for another lover," Magoffin answered cynically. "Life is too short for Josefina to mourn the departure of anyone—not even Plácido,

108

whose competence must be conceded, I think."

The gray, brown, dun, black, and bay mules plodded on. Ross had rejected all white mules, for they were too easily seen from a long distance.

Plácido's was the best mule of the seven hundred; he had picked it with unerring judgment: a coyote dun, a dun with a black stripe down its back. No Mexican ever rejected a coyote dun mule.

The line seemed endless, and the sun grew hot while they waited. There was, of course, no sign of Valeria, but José Cordero came up after a while and reined in his horse. "A great train you have there," he said to Connelly.

"*Gracias*," said Connelly.

"If you can get them through the Comanche wilderness you will have performed a great accomplishment."

"We expect to," said Ross shortly.

Cordero looked at him. Ross was dressed in buckskin pants and shirt, both laced at the front with rawhide; Comanche-style moccasins, and a wide-brimmed felt hat; his two six-shooters were in a wide belt around his waist.

"You seem prepared for the trip," Cordero said, perhaps a little enviously.

"I have been on the Trail before," said Ross.

He jumped down to pull a mule out of the file and tighten its girth strap, then led it back into line. "We'll lose some packsaddles the first few days," he told Connelly, "until the mules get tired of fighting them."

"Just so you don't lose the silver out of them," said Magoffin.

"No chance of that."

Another party came up with Dr. Jennison and Governor Irigoyen. The governor had a satisfied smile on his thin face. "I am very happy to see them actually under way," he said. "This is a great day for Chihuahua."

The rear guard of the dragoons came into sight, led by Lieutenant Tapia, who was not quite as struttily dressed as Esquibel but nevertheless sat his fine bay gelding very smartly.

"That horse won't last three days in the desert," said Magoffin. "Too thin."

"We've got forty extra mules," said Ross. "He'll be glad to trade before we reach Paso."

The last mule plodded past them. The twenty dragoons under Tapia pranced by on fine horses; whatever else they lacked, they were beautifully mounted.

The crowd, following the end of the train, surged in behind it. Ross turned to Connelly and shook hands.

"Good luck," said Connelly.

Ross grinned. "See you back in Chihuahua in four months."

"Better make it five," said Magoffin, shaking hands.

Irigoyen shook hands also, and patted him on the shoulder.

Ross started for the front of the train, Hermenijildo behind him. At the first cross street he left the train, motioning Hermenijildo to continue. It was a long chance, he knew, but he rode back to the square and past the Sierra house. He looked up and saw Valeria on the balcony. She must not have recognized him at once, but he took off his hat and swept it low before him, and he heard her golden laugh. *"Buena suerte, señor,"* she said, and he rode past her window and galloped back to the train.

"Was she waiting?" asked Hermenijildo.

Ross stared at him.

"I sent word to her," said Hermenijildo.

Ross nodded. "And what of Chonita?"

"We have said our good-byes. She suffers from the morning sickness and so she did not come."

"So you're really going to be a father!"

Hermenijildo said, without changing expression, "It was to be expected."

When they camped that night there were a dozen fires. Some men were guarding the mules; others cooked deer meat and tortillas; some made coffee. While they were eating, Ross made the rounds of the camp. Lieutenant Tapia's men were at one end of the campground; Esquibel's were at the other. As Ross walked through Esquibel's camp, he sensed something wrong. He went back. Esquibel himself was eating at a fire with Hermenijildo, Apolinar, Andrés, Tapia—an officers' mess.

Ross went and counted Esquibel's men. Then he went to the fire where Esquibel was eating. "You started with thirty soldiers in your detail," he said abruptly.

Esquibel eyed him over a cup of coffee. *"Sí, señor."*

"And you now have only twenty-five. Where is the big one with the pitted face?"

Esquibel's answer was long enough delayed to be

111

impudent. "I sent a squad of men ahead to Paso," he said, "to notify the commander."

Ross's eyes narrowed. "Who told you to do so?"

Esquibel wiped his mustache. "I used my own judgment," he said.

Ross's eyes narrowed. "You are not in command of this expedition. You are to send out no advance parties unless I order it."

"But, *señor*—"

"That is an order, Captain!"

Finally Esquibel said sulkily, "The governor has told me to be helpful."

"But he did not tell you to betray us," Ross said. "There must be an understanding between us, Captain. Otherwise, you may take your dragoons and return to Chihuahua in the morning."

"What is the understanding?"

"I am in charge. I want no arguments."

Esquibel's eyes hid his thoughts. Finally he said, "Very well, *señor*—if you must be jealous of your position."

Ross left him. Hermenijildo joined him later in the dark. "The captain is going to make trouble," he said.

"I know that."

"Is he in the pay of Mangum, do you think?"

"Or Cordero."

"What did he have to gain by sending a detachment ahead to Paso?"

"He could alert the commander there, and they would be ready to confiscate the gold and silver under the law. No doubt Esquibel, in addition to whatever he's getting from Cordero, would get a percentage of the contraband."

"It is a grave problem. What are we going to do?"

"In the morning," said Ross, "we turn east across the desert to hit the Conchas River. We'll follow that into Presidio, and we won't go anywhere near Paso."

Esquibel started to put up an argument when Ross ordered the caravan to turn east, but Ross gave him no satisfaction. "We go this way," he said. "You may go on to Paso if you wish, since you apparently have friends there."

The river afforded water on the long desert stretches of sand and cactus. The stream was marked by willows and cottonwoods, and, away from the water, by bear-grass that grew on tall stems and was called *palmas* by the Mexicans. It was game country, with black-tailed deer, red deer, antelope out on the prairies, rabbits and quail, wild turkeys sometimes in the trees, and wild hogs in the brush along the stream.

Ross had Apolinar organize a hunting party, for a hundred men required at least two or three antelope or deer every day as meat. The precious stores of flour and corn must be spread as thin as possible in anticipation of delays in the unexplored wilds of northwest Texas—for nobody could be sure what might be encountered there.

The first untoward incident occurred on their fourth day out. The mules were getting broken to the packs; the wagon mules had settled down to work. The fine dust of the desert blew upon them and settled on their hats, in their clothes, in the lines of their faces. It covered the flat-lashed loads in the wagons, for here were no wagon bows and billowing canvas—the wind would have blown it away—but canvas brought down tight over the load and lashed thoroughly with rawhide strips. The long train was beginning to function well, and Ross had ridden ahead to pick out a camping place for the night, when he saw, far across the desert, a small funnel of dust. He watched it for a while; when he saw it coming closer, he turned the gelding and rode out to the southwest. Hermenijildo joined him silently.

It was a lone rider, and Ross galloped toward him. He made out a black horse, and then a man dressed in Mexican finery.

"Andrés!" he shouted.

Andrés' answer came like a croak. *"¡Señor!"*

Ross gave him water from his canteen, and watered the horse from his hat. "You should have had a mule for the desert," he said.

Andrés, still handsome in spite of the layer of dust on his features, grinned. "If I had taken a mule, Papá would have suspected."

"What will he think now?"

"He will know. I left with a small wagon train for Paso, but when I saw your tracks I told them where I was going, and struck out across the desert."

"It's nice to see you, but I can't sanction your coming. Your *papá* would never forgive me."

"I have told him it is my own doing. Besides, I was twenty-one yesterday."

Ross considered. "I can't send you back: that's a certainty. There is too much danger of Indians. You've run that gantlet once and come through. I suppose you'd better go on with us for a while."

"Very good, *señor*." Andrés was all smiles. "You have a job for me, no?"

"There are jobs for all. Do you know anything about a team of mules and a wagon?"

"*Sí, señor.*"

"Then for the present you can take charge of the wagons. Watch the harness; inspect it every night and keep it repaired. Examine the wheels every night and see that the spokes are solid in the felloes. Grease every axle once a week. I want no screeching axles to attract the Indians. Inspect the tongues and the trees every evening. Look to the lashings. When a load has to be unlashed, it is your responsibility to see that the canvas is brought down tight and the ropes fastened so they will not come loose during the day. No man is to be allowed to help himself to supplies of any kind. You will get instructions from me, and I will tell you when to give out supplies and how much to apportion. Think you can remember all that?"

"*Sí, señor,*" Andrés said happily.

"If you fail me, I'll send you back under guard."

"*Sí, señor;* I understand."

"Get that horse watered and fed. Give him a quart of shelled corn. It's in the fourth wagon."

Andrés rode away at a gallop.

Hermenijildo nodded knowingly. "His *papá* will be pleased when it is over."

"Yes." But Ross was not so sure; Don Mauricio had the look of a very stubborn man, and perhaps a man

115

who would not blame his own son if there was some-body else handy. Therefore Ross could expect to take the onus. Not that that worried him very much except as it might affect the expedition. Don Mauricio might have influence with Irigoyen.

He rode on with Hermenijildo, and five miles farther found a wide bend in the river and a good grassy flat that would furnish grass for the mules for one night. There was driftwood for fires, and the river, besides fur-nishing water, formed a good natural bulwark against attack. He did not anticipate trouble from Indians along the river, but in the wilderness a man did not relax his guard.

The next day Apolinar galloped back from his hunt with a white face. "There is a man around the bend of the river—dead."

Ross looked at him, wondering. A dead man was nothing new to any Mexican. He turned the gelding downstream.

His first impression was of hundreds of buzzards—some red-headed, some black. They sat on the ground and in a cottonwood tree until the branches were about to break, and on a small sod hut near the river. Ross rode up, striking among them with his short-handled whip. They rose heavily and flapped out of reach. "Don't waste shots on them," said Ross.

He found the body on its back before the hut. An arrow still stuck up from the chest. "Mescalero," said Ross. "See the blood channels between the three feathers."

"Bury him," Ross said gruffly. Why a man should

come out here into the wilderness to make a home was hard to know. He dismounted and turned the reins over to Hermenijildo. "I'll see what I can find out in the 'dobe," he said.

He walked over first to look at the body. He had been repelled by the gruesome condition of the corpse, and he feared he might have missed some clue. He looked again, and frowned. "Hermenijildo!" he said in a low voice. "Do you see it?"

"¿Señor?"

"The face! The mustache! It's Bigote Doblado—black and white. Diego Olivarez!" His voice dropped to a whisper. "He saved my life, Hermenijildo." For a moment he stood, looking down at what was left of the man's body. The Mexicans coming up with shovels stopped, watching him.

He remembered Diego smiling in the plaza, explaining his name, refusing a gratuity. He remembered the man rushing into the dueling place where peons well might fear to tread, giving him the warning that had saved his life. Momentarily Ross closed his eyes. Diego had wanted freedom—a little piece of land of his own, a place where he could be a man. A few days ago he had been happy and smiling with his Carlota and his *niños* and his few possessions, and now—this.

Ross stood up and looked to the north, toward Texas and the Comanches. "God damn those dirty, stinking redskins!"

He stood there for a moment, his jaws hard. A hesitant voice asked, "*Señor*, shall we dig now?"

Ross looked down again and drew a deep breath. "Dig!" he said, and turned away.

He went to the hut, expecting to find the bodies of Carlota and the children, but he should have known better. He found scraps of clothing, a woman's cotton dress, brush-torn, patched with thorns; the children, too, were gone. To judge by the marks of bare feet, there had been four of them. The woman and the children would be captives; the children would be beaten and brutally treated; if they were too young, and cried, they would be killed. The woman—it was the usual thing when Indians captured a woman. Their homicidal energy on a raid seemed to turn into sexual energy as soon as they captured a woman. Ross shook his head grimly.

Carlota. He remembered her well. A smiling, intelligent, friendly face. A proud girl—and a girl to be proud of. And he remembered that Diego *had* been proud. A woman who had little of material things, but very much of the things of the spirit.

He finished examining the hut. In a corner opposite the fireplace, a cheap colored lithograph of Christ on the cross had been mounted on the tall stump of a cottonwood tree, about the height of his head, and through it a tomahawk had cut a deep gash diagonally.

Ross went out. "They're gone," he told Hermenijildo.

"What can we do, *señor?*"

"He saved my life," said Ross. "the least we can do is find her and rescue her from the savages. But I do not know how."

He signaled to one of his Tonkawas, who had come in silently. The Indian rode up.

"*Hecula?* Who?"

The Tonkawa, with no expression on his dark face but that of watchfulness, said, "Moccasins turned up at toes."

"That's Mescaleros, all right," said Ross. "How many?"

"The Tonkawa shrugged and held up both hands, fingers spread.

Ross nodded. "How long ago?"

The Indian pointed at the sun, described an arc back across the sky to the east, where the sun had risen, then back up again to the zenith.

"Yesterday about noon," Ross said. "From the looks of the body, that's about right."

"We can organize a party to rescue the mother and children," said Hermenijildo.

But Ross shook his head. "We'd never catch them. If it was a small party they would move fast, and by this time they're probably back in Texas, miles away. Second place, we've got our job cut out for us: delivering this train to Arkansas. For all we know this could be a trap to split us up. I don't say it is, but it could be. They might be just waiting for us to divide our men."

"I didn't know," said Apolinar, who had also come up, "that the Indians were capable of such strategy."

"Some are. Old Muke-war-rah of the Penateka Comanches is a very clever chief, and quite capable of such trickery. Likewise, I wouldn't put it past him to make his braves wear Mescalero moccasins just to fool us. I feel sure this is Comanche work."

"What difference would it make?" asked Hermeni-jildo. "They're both Indians."

"It makes considerable difference," Ross said. "If we assume it's a small party of Mescaleros, we would expect them to head back home to the hills of New Mexico, and we wouldn't be worried; whereas if they're Comanches they're the most dangerous tribe in Texas, for they are many and they are aggressive. Likewise, it is nothing for them to travel far from home and be gone for months at a time. So if it was Comanches, the desert might be full of them and we'd never know it." He nodded at Tonkawa, and the Indian turned and went away silently. "Pass the word through the train," he said, "so nobody will get careless."

"I am feel very sad about the woman and children," said Hermenijildo.

Ross watched the men shoveling dirt in on the mangled body of Diego. He said harshly, "We'll get the girl back sometime, somehow."

Chapter 10

Presidio del Norte was a miserable hamlet of a dozen or so mud huts clustered around the presidio, a heavily walled fort within which was the inevitable Catholic church. The town itself was on a gravelly hill overlooking the junction of the Conchas and the Rio Grande—which latter was called, at that point, the Puercos, because of its muddy waters.

Their long train rolled in to the wide-eyed amazement of men, women, and children. Apolinar had gone ahead to get permission to camp, and he conducted the train through the little town and onto a grassy shelf where they could camp for the night.

Ross, flanked by Hermenijildo and Captain Esquibel, went to call on Lieutenant Oconor, an astonishingly young man who offered them brandy. "It isn't what you are used to," he said, pouring it. "It comes from Paso up the river, however, and is our best native brandy."

Ross visited Señor Don Lawreano Paez, the Mexican customs officer, and told him they expected to be back in four or five months with goods, and was assured that Don Lawreano had already received communication from Irigoyen in regard to the matter. Don Lawreano very discreetly manifested no curiosity about the cargo being taken out of the country, and Ross found that up to that time Don Lawreano had never had an opportunity to give a customs certificate for any imported goods.

That night most of the *arrieros* and drivers went into town to find pulque and females and to celebrate with whatever facilities the town afforded. It was late when Andrés finally got together a crew to grease the wagon axles. They could have gone a few days more, but this was the seventh day, and Andrés seemed set on carrying out his orders implicitly, so Ross said nothing against it.

Hermenijildo sought out Ross. "I have seen the big one with the pitted face who went to Paso. Does it mean trouble, *señor?*"

"Nothing else," Ross said grimly.

The first *arrieros* to spend their few coins were back soon after dark, not too sober. Nevertheless Andrés corralled them. He piled up rough-hewn planks and used a spare tongue to pry each wheel off the ground. While two or three men held the end of the lever down, two others took off the wheel, cleaned out the mixture of dirt and grease with their bare hands, and repacked the axle with clean grease.

During this process the repackers were in no hurry, and there was considerable badinage between them and the men holding the lever. "Why did you come back so early?" asked one. "Did you run out of money?"

"I didn't need money," said the man sitting on the lever. "The woman liked me—but her husband came home and found us in bed."

Ross walked closer. The pile of blocking looked wobbly in the center. One man was holding the wheel upright while another was scooping out the dirty grease with his fingers and snapping it to the ground.

"Why did *you* come home so early?" the man asked without looking up.

"I drank up all the pulque," said the man on the end of the lever.

Andrés jumped toward him. "*¡Cuidado!*"

But the *arriero,* demonstrating the fact that he had imbibed copiously, swayed, and then lost his balance. He sprawled full length on his face in the dirt, and the lever, relieved of his weight, arose abruptly. Six feet from the ground it tossed the other two men off and shot almost vertical. The corner of the wagon came down with a crash, impelled by the weight of four thousand pounds of food. A woman's voice rose in a scream, followed by a man's low growl.

Andrés shouted, "*¡Burros! ¡Jumentos!*" and gave the men a tongue lashing in Spanish that would have done credit to any *arriero* in the business. Ross was about to tell him it was enough when he saw tears in the young man's eyes, and refrained.

He put a hand on Andrés' arm. "Get more blocking," he said. "Get the axle back into the air, and there's no harm done. Just see that the dirt is cleaned off."

Relief had never been more apparent on anyone's face than on Andrés'. "*Sí, señor,*" he said fervently, and began to shout orders.

Ross went to the wagon, examined the lashings on the corner that had fallen, threw back a rope, grasped a corner of the canvas, and lifted it high. In the light reflected from the campfire of mesquite roots he saw the brown face of Plácido, and beside him, on a pile of blankets, was Josefina, wide-eyed and scared.

"*Señorita.*" Ross bowed. "I do not seem to have seen you since the night in the Nine Cats."

"*No, señor,*" she said in a whisper.

He looked at Plácido. "so you've kept her here in this little nest for all this time." He shook his head. "It must have been a difficult trip, *señorita,* under this hot canvas."

She said nothing.

"But then the exhaustion of making love all night possibly closed your eyes in slumber during the day."

Still she did not answer, but drew closer to Plácido.

There was quite a crowd around them now, and Josefina shrank still closer to Plácido.

"I have no control over your habits," Ross said to Plácido, "but the teams have had to pull this woman, and you have had to feed her from our supply. I shall take it out of your pay."

Plácido did not seem greatly disturbed by this news. "*Sí, señor,*" he said.

"And she will have to stay in Presidio."

"But, *señor*—"

"There will be no argument, *hombre.*"

Plácido muttered, "*Sí, señor.*"

"Now get out of there."

"But, *señor*—"

"Get out!"

Plácido climbed out sullenly. He reached back in and got his straw hat. "*Señor,* if Josefina stays in Presidio, I stay, too."

"If you do, you will end up in the *juzgado* at Chihuahua, for you made a deal with me and I gave you money for your family before we left."

Plácido glowered at him and backed away.

"*Señorita,*" said Ross, "I shall have to ask you to give up your quarters in the wagon."

She climbed out slowly, making no effort to conceal her bare thighs in the firelight.

"I don't know where you will go," he said, "but I have no doubt you will be able to make your way in Presidio as well as in Chihuahua."

He turned to look at the men who had been thrown

off the lever. The man who had been on the end, San-tiago, was following Josefina's movements with a gleam in his eyes. "Are you hurt?" Ross asked.

Santiago seemed to pull himself out of the clouds with an effort. "No, *señor,* I—that is, I have lost two teeth." He threw back his head and showed a bloody gum.

Ross scrutinized it. "Did the whole teeth come out?"

"We found both of them," said the one who had been cleaning out the wheel hub.

"All right, get this thing back up in the air and finish the job."

"*Señor,*" said Santiago, "I must get a drink."

Ross watched Josefina walk away with a swing to her hips. "You will stay on your job. You can get a drink later."

They forded the Rio Grande on its limestone bed; the water was not deep from the mountain snows in the Santa Fe district, for those snows had not yet begun to melt. They crossed the range of mountains immediately north of the river and descended into the desolate wilderness of mountains and desert that led to the Pecos.

A more broken country was hard to imagine. Ross had his Tonkawa scouts out far ahead, and he himself rode widely to find camping places and to locate routes by which they would be able to take the wagons. The country was not only mountainous but rugged; many of the canyons were deep gashes cut straight down into the red earth, and he rode onto them suddenly out of a monotonous prairie of spider-like ocotillo and dusty greasewood and odoriferous creosote bush, which the Mexicans called *hediondilla,* or stinking bush. Sometimes the gelding would almost step off the edge of a chasm before it saw it. Most of the canyons were dry at the bottom, and water holes were far apart and hard to find.

The journey to the Pecos was not far but it was arduous. There was little game, but occasionally an eagle soared high in the cloudless sky; there were a few rabbits and rats, and of course thousands of rattlesnakes.

On top of the mountains were vast towns of prairie dogs, which the Tonkawas called *yacoxana-as,* but these were little help for food, for they were too hard to shoot. Grass, too, was scarce, and twice on the way to the Pecos Ross doled out feedings of shelled corn in place of forage. The animals began to show the effects of the heat and lack of feed and water; their ribs became evident, and they were harder to drive and slower to cover a day's journey, while the tempers of the men shortened under the heat of the sun.

They were plagued with trouble. A wheel broke against a stone, and Andrés was desolate. A squad of men from Esquibel's detachment, holding back a wagon on a steep hill by means of rawhide ropes, let it get away; the tongue was split and a mule got a broken hip and had to be shot. A doubletree broke ahead of a spanner; and Ross, beginning to suspect these happenings were not all accidental, examined the tree.

Hermenijildo was at his elbow.

"Do you see what I see?" asked Ross.

"The wood was whittled at the bolt," said Hermenijildo gravely.

"There is no longer any doubt that we have a traitor with us," Ross said, "and I know who he is."

"*Señor*—not Captain Esquibel!"

"Why not?"

"He is of the military," said Hermenijildo.

"Military be damned!" said Ross.

"You are speaking of me, *señor?*" asked a suave voice.

Ross turned. Esquibel stood, feet apart, hands loose, his wide belt carrying two seven-shot pistols. Ross said, "I never noticed you were so well armed before."

"A good soldier," said Esquibel, his black eyes sharp, "always has forces in reserve."

Ross's eyes began to narrow. "Are you ready to commit yourself, then?"

Esquibel shrugged elaborately. "Oh, no, *señor*. I merely came to inquire about the delay."

Ross pointed to the whittled doubletree. "I'm sure you know as much about it as I do. Whose money paid for it—Cordero's?"

Esquibel looked very sad. "I am sure I know nothing of what you speak."

"You know enough," Ross said grimly, "and I am going to hear it from you or take you apart with my bare hands."

Esquibel smiled. "I regret to point out, *señor*, that you have only a knife and pistol, while I have two pistols. Perhaps you have overlooked this."

Ross took a step toward him. "And you—"

"*¡Señor! ¡Señor!*" Apolinar galloped up and jerked his horse to a sliding stop. "*Señor*, there are men ahead! They have a paper from Don Lawreano Paez!"

Ross frowned. "What kind of papers?"

"They demand to search the train for contraband gold and silver."

Ross swung into the saddle and galloped toward the head of the long train. The mules were standing, cropping the scanty grass, switching at flies. Plácido was sitting indolently on the ground in the shade of his coyote dun. A group of Mexicans in the usual motley dress of either outlaws or army men were arrayed in a line across the line of march. Ross rode up to them. "Who is the spokesman here?" he demanded.

A peon in a big straw hat said defiantly, "I am the *mayordomo, señor.*"

Ross looked at him. He was the big man with the pitted face. "Are you from Don Lawreano?"

"*Sí, señor;* here is my paper." He handed Ross a small rectangle of heavy rag paper printed on one side. Ross glanced at it. "To search for suspected items carried without legal permit," it said. Ross looked at the man. "Can you read?"

The man moistened his lips. "No, *señor,* I do not read. I am only—"

"Does this man give you trouble, Juan?"

Ross turned to look into the insolent face of Esquibel. "These are your men?" Ross said quickly.

Esquibel shrugged. "They are under my orders."

"Are they soldiers?"

"Of course, *señor*."

"Very good. Hermenijildo!"

"*Sí, señor*."

"Take down the name of every man in this group. I want Conde to know what soldiers he has on his payroll."

Juan backed away, his eyes wide. "I do not want to be in the army, *señor*." He looked pleadingly at Esquibel. "*Capitán*—"

Esquibel was taken aback for a moment. Then he said: "These men are under Don Lawreano. They have an order to search the mules."

Ross turned to Juan and the ragged-looking men behind him. "*Bien, hombres*. Who will be first to open a saddlebag?"

Juan moistened his lips, looked at Ross, and backed away.

Esquibel shouted. "Do your duty! *¡Adelante!*"

Juan still backed away, shaking his head.

Ross turned to Esquibel. "Captain, your men refuse to search the train. Apparently they believe the cargo is satisfactory."

Esquibel compressed his lips, looked at the cowering men, and then at Ross. "You damn' Yanqui," he snarled, and suddenly drew a pistol. "*¡Arriba!* Put your hands up, *señor*, or I shall blow your head off!"

Ross laughed. "That's the wrong pistol," he said. "That one isn't loaded."

He saw the faint look of uncertainty in Esquibel's eyes, and that was enough. He plunged forward to his right. Esquibel pulled the trigger, but the pistol misfired. Ross, with his hand on his six-shooter, said, "Will you draw the other one, Captain?"

Esquibel was caught in his own trap. If he had carried out his bluff, and been successful, he could have retired to the Sandwich Islands and lived like a millionaire. But now he might have to go back and face Irigoyen with very little in the way of explanation. He had no way of knowing why the pistol had misfired. Perhaps, as Ross had suggested . . . deliberately, he drew the other pistol.

Ross shot him through the point of the breastbone. Esquibel was smashed backward, and went down. Ross reloaded his pistol and said to Hermenijildo and Apolinar: "I ask you to certify that Esquibel said he was in charge of these men who were to search the train, and that he drew first. *¿Verdad?*"

Hermenijildo nodded.

"We saw it," said Apolinar, staring at the body.

Ross put the search warrant in his pocket and turned to Hermenijildo. "Get this coyote buried. Notify Lieutenant Tapia he is in charge of all the dragoons. Give these men some corn and send them back to Presidio."

"*Sí, señor.*"

Ross glanced at the dead captain. "That's one level disposed of," he said, and picked up the two pistols from the ground. He handed them to Apolinar. "Get the train going!" he said. "We've wasted too much time on this *jumento* already. If he'd had half as much brains as he had ambition, we would be dead and he would be on the road to California."

All day long the huge mule train wound up and

down over the hills, in and out and across the canyons, through passes, across open sand. The seven hundred mules and seven wagons raised a tower of dust that could be seen for fifty miles, and there was evidence that the Comanches were watching it, for Apolinar failed to find deer for the second day in a row, and instead brought in two javelinas, or wild hogs. "I have great sorrow, *señor*," he said earnestly, "but I and my men cannot seem to find enough game, except for these pigs, which are hard to locate."

"Keep trying," said Ross. "Give your horses a feed of corn every morning, for they've got to keep going."

He looked at the boy, and barely restrained a grin, for Apolinar looked like anything but a young Mexican dandy. All three Mexican young men had adopted buckskin clothing as soon as their own wore out, and now they wore moccasins and felt hats and, with their brown skins, were indistinguishable from Indians at a short distance. They pleased Ross, for they were the best assistants he had ever had. Hermenijildo watched constantly at Ross's elbow, ready to undertake any job; Apolinar often left camp before daylight and some-times would not come back until almost midnight; and Andrés guarded the seven wagons as carefully as if they had been babies.

A new element tried their patience: the canyons. It began to require too much time to head the canyons, and Ross appointed a squad to cut down the banks and make a way for the wagons. Even then the banks were almost impassably steep, and it required many mules and men to get a wagon across.

The day after Apolinar had reported no game in sight, Ross, riding far ahead and flanked by the Tonkawas at a distance of several miles, saw an antelope start up fully a mile away, circle, and then float off to the west at unbelievable speed.

He called the Tonkawas in at noon and handed out a sack of tobacco to each of them, heard their grunts in thanks. Ross, squatting on his heels, asked, "How is it ahead?"

The leader, a grizzled Indian called Xoyco-okic, the Soft-Shelled Turtle, looked all around them at the vast expanse of brush and at the far-distant horizons. "Long time no rain," he said, "but river not far."

"Is there water in the river?"

"Will be much water." Xoyco-okic looked to the west with age-old eyes that seemed to peer into infinity. "Rain in mountains seven suns ago," he said. "River high when we get there."

Ross had been too much around Indians to question the statement. How Soft-Shelled Turtle could tell it was raining several hundred miles away none but he knew—and possibly not even he, but Ross had not the slightest doubt there would be heavy water in the Pecos when they reached it.

One of the younger Tonks grunted something, and Soft-Shelled Turtle looked at Ross. "You no drink river water. Is bad-salty. Mules die like grasshoppers."

"What will they drink?"

"Fresh water—springs. We find."

"One more thing. You see game run from far away—too far to shoot?"

The old Indian nodded.

"That should not be. It says there are Indians just ahead of us."

"Is so." Soft-Shelled Turtle nodded. "We see sign."

"What kind?"

Soft-Shelled Turtle held a guttural conference with his companions, then said to Ross. "All Penetixka— Comanche. We find sign at water hole. Comanche brave put hands in water, balance on arms, like this"— he demonstrated—"to drink. Leave no sign. Squaw put knees in soft mud. Only squaws have fat knees."

"How do you know they are not Apache?"

"Apaches no take squaws on raiding party. Only Comanches."

Ross got up. "Far ahead?"

"One sun," said Soft-Shelled Turtle.

"*Bueno*. You watch—more careful. You report all signs. Every night I give you more *nexpaxkan*— tobacco. *¿Está bueno?*"

"*Bueno,*" said the Tonkawa.

The Indians camped by themselves, apart from the Mexicans. Tapia's dragoons had a separate mess; the *arrieros* camped apart from the muleskinners, and Ross and his three assistants had their own fire. And that afternoon they stopped early after a good day's trip of some three and a half leagues.

Ross had the big stone *metate* unpacked from one of the wagons, and set two men to grinding corn for tortillas, for Apolinar had come in at noon, very disgusted, with nothing but a half-grown ocelot for meat.

Ross went over to the Indians' camp about dark.

133

"Did you find sign today?" he asked.

Soft-Shelled Turtle nodded slowly. "The tracks go to the Pecos—Horsehead Crossing."

Ross was thoughtful. "You believe they will wait there for us?"

"They sure you will go to Horsehead Crossing; now they go ahead to wait. You have big train, many mules. They like."

"Is the crossing a good place for ambush?"

"Very good," declared Soft-Shelled Turtle. "You go down in river, they up on banks. They shoot many arrows, very fast; take many scalps."

"How many Comanches?"

"Probably many—two, three, four hundred."

"Do you think game will be as scarce across the Pecos?"

"You find buffalo other side. Much meat. Good meat. Not like prairie dog."

Ross smiled. He himself was getting a little tired of soup made with wheat flower and a few joints of prairie dog. "Then where can we cross below the Horsehead?"

Soft-Shelled Turtle's eyes narrowed as he looked into the far distance. "Seven leagues—one good day's march with mules."

"Can we go there directly from here?"

"You go *más allá*—a little farther, around that peak yonder." He pointed. "Then turn right. You find good road in canyon. No water. Good road. Canyon lead to Pecos."

Ross passed out tobacco. "You go that way tomorrow. Find road. We follow."

He went back. The vast emptiness of the semidesert brushland, the silence, the oppressive silence, the heat, the monotony, the lack of water and meat—all these were beginning to have an effect on the men. The only thing that held them together now was the fact that they would be afraid to strike off in small parties through Comanche country.

There were always individual parties of Indians hanging on the flanks of a big train, watching to cut off stragglers. Such Indians were not found in front of a train, because they well knew that every big train sent its best men out ahead; and such parties offered no threat to their change of route, because the main party which wanted to ambush them had drawn off all its warriors to avoid scaring them away from the crossing.

Chapter 11

The grass seemed to grow even poorer. The mules snipped at greasewood and whatever came along. An occasional clump of mesquite trees showed they were nearing a water course, and these were stripped clean of their tiny, symmetrical leaves by the horses.

They watered at a small spring before daylight the next morning. The spring flowed up out of solid rock and filled a hole the size of a barrel. The path down to the water was wide enough for only one at a time, and the narrow canyon below the spring was completely inaccessible, while within a quarter of a mile, at a point where they could get up to the steam bed, the water had sunk into the sand.

Ross watched the slow process of watering seven hundred mules, and warned Plácido and Andrés not to lash packs or harness the animals until all were out, for it would be some time. They had a quarter-moon for the task, which made it easier, and Ross kept the dragoons posted all along the way. He told Tapia: "The guides say the Comanches are waiting for us at Horsehead Crossing. It is good to be very watchful. If they have spies out, they may find that we are changing course, and we can look for trouble."

"*Sí, señor*," said Tapia without apparent feeling.

An hour before sunup the long, long train of mules was watered. "Give them no feed," Ross ordered, "because today they will get no water, and an animal without water will go farther on an empty stomach."

Plácido nodded—almost too agreeably, the fleeting thought came to Ross. But he had other things to think about. He saw that the men filled their canteens and cautioned them against using the water before noon. Twenty miles would be a long day's drive with the mules in no better condition than they were.

He rode ahead with the Tonkawas and picked out a route for the wagons. Back in Chihuahua they had tried to figure out a way of transporting everything in pack-saddles, but bulky items and hard-to-lash items could be transported more easily by wagon—and by one-third as many mules. Besides, they had to have a wagon trace for the return trip with bulky goods.

For four miles they followed along the high edge of

the escarpment. The canyon below was dry; the sides were precipitous, and the growth was mostly salt cedar and greasewood and some mesquite.

When they reached the spot where Soft-Shelled Turtle said they could get into the canyon, Ross looked it over. It was possible, and that was about all. He got a party of Tapia's men to clear out brush and small trees and dig a channel just wide enough for the wagons. They could then tie ropes to a wagon and enlist fifty or sixty men to hold it back. In this way the seven wagons reached the bottom of the canyon, where it was relatively easy going on the stream bed, which was sometimes sand, sometimes gravel. Ross had an extra span of mules put on each wagon, for the pull was long and hard, and the sun at the bottom of the canyon was stifling hot.

He tried to keep the men from using their canteens as long as possible, but by ten o'clock they were dipping into them, and by noon there was not a swallow of water left in any except his own, his three assistants', Tapia's and, oddly enough, Plácido's.

They stopped in the bottom of the canyon for an hour to rest the mules. A few tules or rushes were eaten clean within minutes, but Ross would not allow the mules to be fed or any rations to be given the men. At one o'clock they began to relash the packs. Each *arriero* could get a mule ready to travel in about three minutes, and each man was responsible for ten mules, so a half-hour was required to relash. By that time, of course, Andrés had his wagons on the move, and Plácido himself was a demon of energy.

The long train strung out in the bottom of the canyon and moved forward. Ross was uneasy, for it would be suicidal to get caught in there. But the far-ranging Tonkawas reported no Comanches within several miles, and Ross urged the train on down the canyon.

He rode out ahead, and about six o'clock he found the first water hole. It was another hour before the mules began to arrive, and Ross gave instructions to Plácido to stand there and personally to see that every mule drank his fill, for the water in the Pecos—not far away, according to the Tonkawas—was so heavily loaded with brine that it might very well be fatal, and the mules might smell the water and head for it instead of waiting their turns at the spring. Satisfied that the mules were in good hands, he rode on to the mighty Pecos, where many caravans had come to a tragic end.

It was not a big water, but the sides were steep and in many places vertical, and the red sandstone walls were strewn with boulders. The course of the muddy water was so tortuous that it was difficult to know where to put the train across without actually trying it, so he rode on, watching carefully.

The canyon of the Pecos was, he judged, three to four hundred feet deep at that point, and they might have to turn the wagons downstream to find a way out. But then he saw Soft-Shelled Turtle sitting his bare-backed horse high on the east bank, and rode through the water, which was about belly-deep on the gelding, and found a narrow dry gully which he realized at once could be widened with picks and shovels to permit passage of the wagons. He rode through it and came out on top. He sat his horse there beside Soft-Shelled Turtle and looked over the vast expanse of land to the west—dry, desolate, almost devoid of living creatures. He snapped his whip at a rattlesnake and broke its back, then tossed it over the cliff. It was likely, he thought, that javelinas could be found in the thick brush along the river bottom, because the javelina was not poisoned by the snakes, and fed on them with relish.

"The rain has not reached here," he said to the Indian.

The Tonkawa said calmly, "You found the river a day soon. But"—he pointed with a mahogany-red forefinger—"you see that?"

Ross watched. A few small pieces of driftwood floated around the nearest bend, and after them a few white bubbles. Ross nodded. "It's coming."

"Soon," said Soft-Shelled Turtle.

Ross rode back down the *arroyada* and galloped the black to the spring.

"Lieutenant," he told Tapia, "I want thirty men to widen out a road for the wagons."

"It is late," said Tapia. "We will widen the road tomorrow."

"No. Tonight."

"*¿Señor?*"

"The river is rising."

"I have seen no rain clouds."

"*¡Teniente!*" Ross's voice was sharp. "You are under my orders!"

Tapia looked at him, and Ross saw the light of rebellion begin to glow in the officer's eyes. Tapia had felt his responsibility since the death of Esquibel.

"*Teniente,*" said Ross, "I have in my care a great many men and a great deal of property, some of which belongs to the governor. I should not like to report to him that it was lost through the neglect of an officer of the dragoons."

"But, *señor,* my men have not eaten all day, and they are tired."

"I am not going to argue with you, Lieutenant, but I will point out one thing: you have not traveled much in the West or you would know it is always good policy to cross a stream when you come to it, for many things can happen at night. In this case the first flood waters are already showing in the river. By morning it will be impassable, and then you will see the spectacle of seven hundred mules and a hundred men trapped in the canyon. It might well be," he said after a pause, "that the Comanches now waiting for us at Horsehead Crossing would find us here."

Tapia's eyes widened. "I did not know of these Comanches."

"You do not know of many things. Your business is soldiering, not freighting."

"Very well, *señor.* I will give you your men."

Ross led them across the river and put them to work. By that time the first mules were reaching the river, and he directed the *arrieros* to let them spread out and graze on whatever sparse vegetation they might find. He went back to the *arroyada* and wielded a pick with the rest of them. When he heard a shout, he looked up in time to see thirty mules racing under full pack for the river. He stared for a moment, hardly believing what he saw. Then he caught up the gelding and put it into the water at a gallop. But the water slowed him down, and the mules splashed into the river and lowered their heads to drink. He shouted, and the *arrieros* ran toward the spot. The first *arriero* reached them before Ross, and they both tried to haze two mules back out of the water, but could not. Ross rode one mule down with the gelding, but it would not get up; it went to its knees and then rolled over, the pack still in place.

Ross left it and tried to head off the others. But they were coming in a beeline, and would not be stopped. He saw it was useless. He used his rope and tried to pull one away from the water, but with its legs braced it was heavier than a five-year-old steer.

Within ten minutes all thirty of the mules had filled up on the water, and Ross was hunting Plácido. "I told you to make sure every mule watered at the spring!" he thundered.

Plácido looked scared. "*Sí, señor.* I have done as you ordered."

"Then why did those thirty mules head for the river water?"

Plácido backed a step, fearfully. "I do not know, *señor.*"

Ross was angry. "I know damn' well you know, and I'll find out if I have to beat it out of your hide."

He went back. The mule that had fallen to its knees in the water was still there, its head on the bottom, drowned. A second mule was lying on its side on the sand, gasping. Half a dozen others were lying down. He swore violently.

"But, *señor*," said Hermenijildo, "thirty mules are not so much. The merchants—"

"I don't give a damn what they're worth in cash! I'm concerned with what they're worth to us out here in the middle of the wilderness!"

"I don't understand."

"In Chihuahua we could buy thirty more mules. Out here there is no place to buy. Understand?"

"*Sí*," Hermenijildo said humbly.

They lost twenty-two out of the thirty. The other eight would be all right after a day or two. Ross set men to work butchering the dead mules. Their round steaks, he thought, would be safe enough.

By that time the opposite bank was cut away enough to permit passage of the wagons with care. Ross had kept one eye on the river, which by now was definitely becoming roily with a stronger flow, red silt in suspension, small parcels of driftwood, and considerable white foam on its surface.

He had thrown the Tonkawa spies out at a distance of several miles to guard against surprise by the Comanches, and now, after measuring the width of the newly opened passage with a long wand of tamarisk, cut off with his skinning knife, he mounted the gelding and went back across the stream.

"Wagons go first," he ordered. "Andrés, hitch twelve mules to a tongue. It's fairly steep over there. You'll have some trouble with one turn, for the pull on the chain, coming from away around the bend in the *arroyada*, will throw the wagon into the wall, but the men are cutting it away as much as they can."

"It will soon be pitch black," Andrés pointed out.

"All the better. The Comanches are not likely to attack in blackness. Get going now. We should be over within an hour. Then we'll be able to unharness and prepare some food."

"I have much hunger," Andrés said soberly.

"You'll be fed," Ross promised. "Apolinar brought in nine turkeys a while ago, and they're cleaning them now. Tomorrow, if all goes well, we'll have buffalo hump for supper."

Andrés began to shout orders.

"*Señor*," said Hermenijildo, "I too have much hunger. Could you not issue orders that Apolinar and his men start cooking the meat now?"

Ross shook his head. "We don't dare to make a fire until we have all the animals and goods across and are ready to defend them. Just be sure of one thing: every man should have a full canteen before he crosses, for we don't know how far it will be to water on the other side."

"*Sí, señor.*"

"Plácido!"

"*Sí, señor*," Plácido answered, coming from under a wagon.

"Get your *arrieros* under way. Bring the mules together and prepare to start lashing packsaddles as soon as the fourth wagon is across. We'll camp on the high ground on the other side tonight."

"*¡Teniente!*"

Tapia answered "*Sí*," and appeared out of the blackness, for even the work on the *arroyada* was

143

done by starlight.

"Throw your twenty men out as foragers to guard against a surprise attack from the rear. They will follow the cargo mules across the river."

"*Bien, señor.*"

"And Andrés, as soon as the mill is brought across, have your men set it up and start grinding corn. The men must have a good meal tonight—plenty to eat."

The water had risen several inches by the time the first wagon lumbered into the current, and the mules were nervous, but Ross had Hermenijildo go back into the *arroyada* and start a small fire where it could be seen by the mules but from no other angle, and this helped them into the water and guided them to the other side.

By the time the fourth wagon rumbled across the red sandstone bottom and into the current, Plácido began to shout at his *arrieros,* and they in turn shouted at their mules, and in an incredibly short time the great long string of mules was lined up, each mule finding its own pack and standing there, waiting to be loaded.

The last wagon was no sooner in the water than Plácido's pack mules were ready to follow. The dragoons closed in behind. Normally they would have driven the reserve band of mules, but with the losses from alkali water and the extra animals pulling the wagons, there was no reserve left.

Each wagon struck its side against the wall of the passage at the turn, but they got by, with tremendous scraping of the wheel hubs through the hard red dirt, by the combined pushing and pulling of many men, accompanied by loud and fervent swearing, of which the words were Spanish but the intonations were familiar to teamsters all over the country.

They got the wagons out on fairly level ground east of the river, and arranged them in a semicircle with the open side toward the river. The mules were turned out to crop the short, curly buffalo grass that now appeared for the first time, and Ross arranged relays of night guards to run two hours apiece, each controlled by Apolinar, Hermenijildo, or Andrés. It was somewhat after ten o'clock, and three shifts would bring them to four o'clock and daylight.

Long before the last pack mule crossed the river, the mill was set up, and the sound of its grinding could be heard for a quarter of a mile.

Ross went back across the river to call in the dragoons, and rode across the stream with Tapia. He hoped the lieutenant noticed that the water was over their stirrups by that time.

Santiago, who usually acted as cook, cut up the turkeys and handed out pieces for the men to cook as they would; many of them ate the meat raw. He also handed out thick steaks cut from the dead mules. The cornmeal was apportioned, one cupful to each man, and some of this was mixed with cold water and sugar and eaten raw by those who were in a hurry. Others built small fires from mesquite branches and found flat rocks on which to bake corncakes. Coffee was passed out, and in most cases eight or ten men would get together and boil it in tin buckets, but here and there a man would build a fire by himself and make his own coffee to suit his taste.

It was almost midnight when Ross finally squatted on his heels to gnaw his leg of half-cooked turkey and to gulp down his chunk of cornbread. He had a tin cup of coffee beside him, made from his own canteen, to wash down the cornbread. Suddenly he felt unutterably weary, and he was conscious of the fact that every man there felt the same way. It had been a long, hard drive—twenty miles that day, without water or food. It was enough to tire anyone. And yet, he knew, there was many more such days ahead of them.

All over the camp, by the small, glowing fires, the men ate in famished silence. The night wind did not cool off as it did in the mountains near Chihuahua, and the silence around them was intense. Except for an occasional stamp by the mules, and sometimes a squeal as one mule bared its teeth against another, there was silence—the silence of the Pecos, land of the twisting river, home of prairie dogs and rattlesnakes.

He lifted his cup and blew on it, set it temporarily on his knee to cool, holding it there by the handle, and then he heard, out of the quiet night, a quick flash-fire of Spanish imprecations:

"¡Caramba!"

"¡Qué hombre malo!"

"¡Jumento!"

"!Burro!"

"¡Tortuga!"

"¡Cabrón!"

"¡Hijo de chingada!"

He leaped to his feet at the first words, recognizing Plácido's expression of amazement and indignation. His cup went flying, and his cornbread dropped in the grass as he ran to the wagon from which came the oaths.

Two men were struggling in the fireglow, one in bare feet, the other in boots. Knives flashed in the red light, and the men grunted as they strained against each other. Plácido's back was toward Ross, his splendid muscles bunched, and Ross recognized Santiago's face, contorted with animosity.

Ross raced up, seized Plácido by the shoulders, and flung him back. He heard Plácido hit the ground and turn like a cat to get back on his feet, and then Santiago, his eyes blazing with fury, advanced on Ross with his knife held before his stomach.

Ross kicked him in the groin; then, as the man's hands dropped, he seized him by the shoulders and spun him away. Ross stood, tall and imposing in the firelight, legs widespread, watching both ways. "I said there will be no fighting among my men, and I meant it!" He heard Santiago getting to his feet. "You got enough, *hombre?*" he asked.

Santiago muttered. Plácido was putting away his knife. Ross glared at Santiago. The wild light died in the man's eyes; his eyelids dropped; slowly he thrust the knife back in his waistband.

"Now," said Ross, "what's it about—you two?"

Neither answered.

Ross said, "I never saw you fight over but one thing, Plácido—and that was Josefina." He stopped suddenly and looked at Santiago. "You had words over her in Presidio. *¿Verdad?*"

Still neither answered.

Ross frowned. "But there's nothing to fight about until you get back. We left Josefina in Presidio." He stared for an instant at Plácido's downcast eyes. "Or did we?" he asked suddenly.

He glanced at Santiago, who also looked at the ground. Then he shouted: "Hermenijildo! Apolinar! Andrés!"

They came running—Andrés with food in his hand.

"Search the wagons! Find that little *chingada!*"

She looked bedraggled when she crawled out from under the canvas of the sixth wagon—worn and drawn from the long journey, and Ross could hardly understand, as she stood there blinking in the fireglow, her black hair disheveled, how she could have endured the last week's travels confined in an almost airless nest among the boxes and crates. And yet he was aware, as she stood with her head high and her eyes unashamed, that she was filled with a wild-animal magnetism that was reflected in her posture, her compact build, her bare legs and shoulders, her fearless black eyes.

"Didn't you like it in Presidio, *señorita?*" he asked, not unkindly.

"Plácido was not in Presidio," she said simply.

"So then how does Santiago get into the game?"

She dropped her head.

"Plácido was not enough for you, eh? And yet it was Plácido, wasn't it, who let thirty mules drink bad water while he was getting a canteen of fresh water to you after a long day's travel?" He looked at Plácido and then at Santiago. "I don't know what to do with you two. Obviously Josefina is not faithful to anybody.

148

Obviously, too, we cannot now send her back. So it looks as if she will have to go with us to Arkansas."

Plácido looked up, pleased.

"But one thing," Ross said ominously: "if either one of you fights over her, I will break him over my knee." He stood wide-legged before the fire and looked around him at the crowd, now consisting of nearly every man in camp except the guards. "If any doubts it, let him speak."

One or two moved uneasily, but nobody spoke.

"Feed her," Ross ordered.

One of Tapia's dragoons went eagerly to the fire.

"A woman out here is like a match in a keg of powder," Ross told his assistants, "but we'll have to do the best we can. . . . *Señorita,*" he said. She looked up. "You will have to work your way in a fashion you may not be accustomed to. There is the *metate,* and grinding corn is woman's work. I don't know whether you can grind enough for a hundred men, but you are going to try. And if I catch you shirking, there will be trouble. Maybe," he said, "eight hours of grinding will leave you too exhausted for the men to fight over."

He added thoughtfully, "Or will it?"

Chapter 12

They were under way at daylight the next morning. The packs from the dead mules were redistributed among the reserve mules. But even before they got the wagons rolling, a band of forty-five antelope started up three miles away and circled grace-fully, then floated off down the valley.

"*Berrendos,*" said Apolinar, watching their course.

"*Berrendos,* yes—but why did they start up?"

Apolinar's eyes widened. "Something disturbed them."

"Of course it did—Comanches."

"Do you think?"

"There are no coincidences in Indian country," said Ross. "Nothing just happens. Remember that, and you will live longer. For today I suggest you don't wander far. We still have mule meat. The Tonks will be out about three miles, and you'd better stay about halfway between them and the train."

"But, *señor*—"

"Sometimes," Ross said, "you can hear crows cawing in the distance." He listened, his head tipped to the west. "I heard it about half an hour ago."

"What does that mean?" asked Apolinar.

"An Indian camp. The crows follow it to pick up the refuse. It means the camp moved either last night or early this morning—probably last night, because the Indians are not early risers, contrary to what you may have heard."

"The train will need meat tomorrow."

"And you need your hair tonight when you come in. Now, listen: three men must ride together—no less. Don't get out of sight of the train and don't go far under any circumstances. Understand?"

"*Sí, señor.*"

"No later than tomorrow we'll find buffalo. They'll

move north, but not all of them. And in a few days we'll be out of the range of this band of Comanches, and there'll be nothing to worry about until we hit the Kotsoteka Comanches along the headwaters of the Brazos. All right, go ahead."

Josefina walked by the side of the first wagon. Someone, probably Plácido during the night had cut down a pair of spare moccasins to fit her small feet, and now she walked along in the dust of the train and over the rough ground, seeming quite contented.

Andrés rode up and said to Ross, "She might as well help drive, hadn't she?"

Ross nodded.

Andrés looked at her thoughtfully. "She may get pretty tired grinding all that corn."

Ross smiled. "Don't worry. She'll have half the men in camp waiting for turns to grind corn."

"¡Señor! Do you think so?"

"Knowing Josefina—yes."

Their route was northeast, and the terrain began to straighten out a little. It still wasn't level prairie, but the grass improved, and Soft-Shelled Turtle reported that there would be fresh water within reach of the wagons.

They stopped before noon to rest the mules and to eat, and almost at once the sound of the grinding pestle in the *metate* arose.

Andrés seemed concerned. "She can't grind much corn in an hour or two," he said.

"Let her go. Our mules carried her for two weeks. It won't hurt her to work a little in return."

"But she's a woman, *señor.*"

Ross grinned. "Never mind. When you're as old as I am you'll know that women bear up under these conditions better than men."

They moved on soon, for there was no water at their stopping place, and the canteens were empty as soon as they finished eating.

Ross rode ahead. The Tonkawas were fanned out in advance on horseback, but a man never could tell where they were until he stumbled on them. About three o'clock in the afternoon he recognized the peculiarly shaped low hill that Soft-Shelled Turtle had described as a landmark. They were to swing around to the northwest of the hill, and on the northeast side they would find a small spring. He studied the country for a moment and determined there was no other such hill in the vicinty. He caught sight of Apolinar and two men riding a mile to the east. All this country was open, and it seemed utterly impossible that an Indian could hide behind the scattered clumps of grass. And yet the Tonkawas were out there somewhere with horses.

He leaned forward in the saddle to send the gelding ahead, but then he sat back hard, suddenly, for ahead of him, not over four hundred yards away, on the top of the small hill, stood an Indian.

He wore no feathers. His face was mahogany black and his hair was braided down the side. He was naked from the waist up, and wore breechclout, deerskin leggins, and moccasins. His arms were at his sides, his bow strung over his back.

Ross looked back. He fired a shot from his six-shooter, and then, knowing that Tapia's advance guard had seen him, turned the gelding and rode in a small circle.

The Indian didn't move. Ross rode slowly toward him, watching the skyline with great care, but he saw nothing move.

Apolinar was closing in at a gallop, and, when he was near, Ross went forward at a trot. He stopped the gelding within twenty feet of the Indian and held his right hand up, palm out, about the height of his shoulder; moving it rapidly from side to side, he gradually raised it higher.

The Indian watched with the insolence typical of the Comanche dealing with whites. Then he said, in good Spanish, "I am Ish-a-ro-yeh, second chief to Muke-war-rah."

"Are you alone?"

"I am alone."

"You've been watching us for days. What do you want?"

"Muke-war-rah want talk—trade."

"We have no trade goods."

The Comanche waved a short, muscular arm at the train. "You have many, many *mulas*. Must have goods. You do not bring this *mulas* all the way from Chihuahua to eat buffalo grass."

"No goods," Ross repeated firmly. "Some food for ourselves. No goods. White iron only."

Apolinar rode up behind him and stopped.

"The chief Muke-war-rah no believe that story. He has watched this *mulas* many days."

"I know," said Ross. "From Presidio del Norte."

Ish-a-ro-yeh looked at him without change of expression. "You know this?"

"We are not men with eyes in the backs of their heads," Ross said scornfully.

"What are you doing in Comanche country?"

Ross had to be careful, for any mention of Texas would infuriate the Comanches. "We are traveling peacefully. We carry the white iron to Arkansas to buy goods. We kill only enough game to eat."

"You are not Mejicano."

"No," said Ross. "I am Anglo." Anything but Texan.

"Muke-war-rah has much to trade."

"We need nothing." Ross waved at the plodding train behind him. "We have clothing."

"You have little *har-ne-wis-ta*—corn."

"True." Ross made it sound deprecatory. "But we are hunters."

"You have found little game."

"True. But last night we killed twenty-two mules, and this morning we had a great plenty of meat. And soon we shall be on the buffalo range, and not even the Comanches can scare away all the buffalo."

"Muke-war-rah has much to trade."

Ross said patiently, "We have not come to trade."

"You carry white iron to Arkansas, huh?"

"Muke-war-rah does not want white iron, and he does not have pans and cloth and needles and knives that we shall get in Arkansas."

The Indian said imperturbably, "Muke-war-rah has other things you not get in Arkansas."

"Not whisky?"

The Indian scowled. "Comanches no trade for whisky."

"Then what?"

"Captives."

It hit Ross with a shock. "Captives!"

"Two *to-a-chee*—children." Ish-a-ro-yeh held up two fingers. "One *wy-e-pe*—woman."

Ross heard an exclamation from Apolinar behind him, but Ross controlled himself and said firmly, "We have nothing to trade for captives."

"You talk—Muke-war-rah."

Ross shook his head. "We are behind schedule now."

Apolinar said in his ear. "*Señor*, he said a woman captive."

"I heard him," said Ross. "But if we act eager we'll never get a chance. Anyway, we are here on business—not to rescue captives."

"You talk Muke-war-rah?" the Indian repeated.

Ross looked back as if considering it. Finally he said, "We'll talk, but we have not much time."

"I come after while. Take you see Muke-war-rah, great chief all Comanches."

Ross nodded as if reluctant. "After while."

He turned back. The foremost mules were within a quarter of a mile, and Plácido had stopped them. He motioned them on and turned back. Ish-a-ro-yeh had disappeared.

"He did it right in front of my eyes," Apolinar said incredulously.

Ross pointed to the left. "See the magpie get up and start scolding. Our friend is going in that direction. He

155

probably has a horse cached down in a draw some-where."

He led the train to the spring three miles farther on, saw that the animals were watered and the canteens filled, and told the men to go ahead with supper.

Half an hour later, without warning, Ish-a-ro-yeh appeared on the slope. The mules near him snorted and reared and wheeled and ran away.

The Indian, followed by three younger braves—two of them no more than fourteen—walked to the fire where Ross was still broiling a strip of mule meat. Ross noted that the Indian was short and heavily built, and walked as if he were not accustomed to it—almost clumsily. It was a characteristic, Ross knew, of these Indians, who of all Indians in America had become horse Indians, and lived and moved and fought and some said loved on horseback. And yet Ish-a-ro-yeh managed to give dignity to his odd walk. He came to the fire with his bow on his back and said, "We go now."

Ross looked around him and saw the tense faces, the hands moving toward rifles. "We go pretty soon," he said. "You like *pa-ha-ma*—tobacco?"

That of course was an unnecessary question, but it gave Ish-a-ro-yeh a chance to nod, and Ross pulled a cloth sack of tobacco from inside his buckskin shirt and handed it to the Indian, who took it gravely. He squatted by the fire, the muscles bulging on his calves and thighs, and set to work to roll a cigarette.

"Coffee?" asked Ross.

"*Hah.*"

Ross said to Plácido, "Get the chief a cup."

But it was Josefina who sprang to her feet, got a clean cup, poured it full of coffee, and handed it to Ish-a-ro-yeh.

He looked at her over the cup as he put it to his lips to see how hot it was, and Josefina, for once abashed by a man's thoroughly frank stare, flushed and turned away.

"You have left your horses?" asked Ross.

Ish-a-ro-yeh grunted: "Back yonder."

Ross said, in Spanish: "I want you, Hermenijildo, and you, Andrés, to go with me. Apolinar, you will watch the guard over the animals. Be doubly careful. At the least relaxation the Comanches will stampede the entire band and we shall be afoot. Remember—a Comanche can go through the grass with less disturbance than a snake." He made the familiar sign-language motion for "Comanche"—fingers together, hand drawn back and to the right in a wavering motion.

Ish-a-ro-yeh looked up and grinned. He had understood, of course, but it made no difference.

"You see," said Ross, taking the strip of mule meat off of the sharpened stake, "he knows as well as I do what we are talking about. It is a game," he said. "Each of us knows what the other will do if he gets a chance, and we are both looking for that chance. Nevertheless," he warned, "it is a deadly game, for lives are the stakes, and he would murder every one of us as cheerfully as he rolls a cigarette—especially with seven hundred mules as a side bet."

He finished his meat. Ish-a-ro-yeh had smoked the cigarette. Ross got up and went for his horse. He gave instructions to Plácido and Tapia. To Andrés and Hermenijildo he said, "Since he has captives, it's not too risky, for he wants to sell them. We can always pretend to think it over and get out of his camp alive."

Down in a draw the Comanches had mounted. Two of them were on paint ponies, the third on a mule-striped dun, and Ish-a-ro-yeh rode a fine chestnut stallion that most certainly had come from some Mexican ranch. They rode out to the west, and the immediate transformation of the Indians was astonishing. Once on horseback, each almost seemed a part of the horse itself. The apparent clumsiness or ungainliness completely disappeared.

"That is why," said Ross, "these fellows are so hard to fight."

They rode west for an hour and a half, and Ross saw no sign of an Indian camp; but suddenly they came out on the edge of a great cliff, and down below them was a green valley filled with hundreds of buffalo-hide teepees. Ish-a-ro-yeh grunted. "Muke-war-rah camp," he said.

Ish-a-ro-yeh led the way down the cliff on a narrow trail.

"Is Muke-war-rah really chief of all the Comanches?" asked Hermenijildo.

"Chief of the Southern Comanches—as much as any chief, I suppose. The Comanches have a very loose organization, like all Indians. Nobody is obliged to render loyalty to any chief—let alone whole tribes or divisions."

They came out on a level meadow at the bottom. The

valley ran east and west, and the sun still shone, an hour above the horizon. They rode silently through the sprawling camp. Dogs yapped and followed them and snapped at the heels of the horses. Heavy-set squaws and round-eyed children watched them suspiciously while Ish-a-ro-yeh wound his way through the scattered teepees, which were placed without rhyme or reason. One of the younger Comanches watching turned abruptly on a dog barking at his heels and launched a sudden kick. The dog's yapping changed instantaneously into a high-pitched broken howling, almost like that of a sobbing child, and Ross, from the corner of his eyes, saw the dog writhing in the dust. He rode on with his eyes straight ahead.

They stopped before a large teepee with the flap thrown back. In front of the teepee was a smoldering fire over which, from a tripod of sticks, hung a big brass kettle. Around the fire, smoking pipes, were five Comanches, all with braided hair, and all but one naked from the waist up. The sun would soon be down at the west end of the valley, and one, older than the rest, had already pulled a blanket around his shoulders. They looked up without apparent interest as the little caravan stopped.

The one nearest the teepee, however, continued to stare into the fire, puffing his pipe occasionally and seeming to be totally unaware of the arrival. Ish-a-ro-yeh broke out in fast, fluid Comanche. The older man, whose face showed the seams of many winters of cold wind and snow and many summers of hot sun and blistering wind and driving sand, answered Ish-a-ro-yeh in a low voice. The other three watched and nodded.

Ish-a-ro-yeh asked a question, and the old man nodded. Ish-a-ro-yeh dismounted and gave a curt signal to Ross, who also dismounted.

He said to Hermenijildo: "Andrés and I will get down. You stay on your horse and hold our reins unless they insist on your getting down. In that case, keep your firearms handy. Ish-a-ro-yeh here understands enough Spanish to know what I am saying, but it doesn't make any difference." He was speaking fast so that Ish-a-ro-yeh would have trouble following him. He handed the reins to Hermenijildo and watched Andrés do the same.

Ish-a-ro-yeh said, "My man take your horses to eat grass."

Ross said firmly: "Our horses are well fed with *har-ne-wis-ta*. They will stay here with us, for they are not used to being pastured." This, of course, was not true, but he had to say something to keep the horses close and at the same time admit no fear.

Ish-a-ro-yeh grunted. He dropped the bridle that was tied around his horse's underjaw and walked through the group sitting around the fire. He went to the brass kettle, picked up a stick lying on the ground, fished out a piece of boiled meat, and ate it wolfishly with his hand. He looked back at Ross, pointed at the kettle, and grunted.

Ross walked forward. The stench of bodies seldom washed but plentifully smeared with oil or tallow that became rancid within hours was almost overwhelming. It was distinctive with the Comanches as it was with many tribes that lived in areas where water was scarce.

The oil kept their skins from drying out and at the same time collected dirt and dust which could be rubbed off later. But it invariably created a characteristic odor. Ross controlled his first instinctive reaction of distaste and followed Ish-a-ro-yeh to the kettle. He dug a piece of well-boiled meat out of the simmering stew and ate it. Andrés stood back and waited; Hermenijildo remained mounted. The taste was good, and except for the lack of salt he was glad to set his teeth in it. What it was he had no idea—buffalo, wolf, javelina. The original meat flavor had all been boiled out.

While he was eating, he estimated the number of teepees as unobtrusively as possible, and counted around four hundred. This meant probably two thousand Comanches in the camp, about eight hundred of whom would be warriors. Such a force could overwhelm his train and wipe them all out if they decided to do so.

Ish-a-ro-yeh finished his meat, wiped his greasy fingers on his buckskin leggings, and sat down. He pulled out the sack of tobacco and began to roll a cigarette. The man nearest the tent flap, who had not until then looked up, raised his head and grunted.

Ross reached inside his shirt, pulled out another sack of tobacco, and handed it to the chief, who took it without looking up. He was a big man even sitting down—outstandingly large for a Comanche, who usually were not over five and a half feet.

He began to roll a cigarette. Ross produced four more sacks and handed them to the silent braves around the fire. Some grunted, some said nothing.

Ish-a-ro-yeh jabbed a mahogany-black thumb toward the big man. "Muke-war-rah, great chief of all Comanches," he said.

The big man raised his eyes at last, and Ross felt as if somebody had run a sharp knife-blade down his spine. The face was intelligent, but the eyes were evil in their unplumbed depths. Ross continued to stare at him, unblinking, until Muke-war-rah reached for a twig to light his cigarette.

Chapter 13

"You have come to ransom our captives," Muke-war-rah said in excellent Spanish.

"No. We have come to visit you, at your request."

Muke-war-rah nodded, a tinge of sarcasm showing in his dark face. "You have much goods."

"As I told your chief, we have no goods for trade. We have only enough for our own use, and the white iron we are going to use for trade."

"White iron is no good to us," said Muke-war-rah insolently. "When we go to the towns of the *to-e-titch-e,* we can get all the goods we want without white iron."

"Then you have no need to trade with us."

Muke-war-rah said, unabashed: "Is not so. We have just returned from Mexico, and our horses are all trotted down."

"We have nothing you want," Ross repeated.

"You have corn. My people do not raise corn. We are too busy fighting."

It was a typical Indian remark. "We have only corn enough for our own use," Ross said.

"You have powder and lead. We need powder and lead, for the new many-shoots guns take much powder and lead."

Ross shook his head firmly. "We have enough only to kill Indians."

Muke-war-rah glanced at him. "You talk like a Comanche."

"We have come far, and shall go farther, and it is no secret that we are well armed and ready to kill Indians at the slightest excuse. If we are allowed to go in peace, we shall keep our rifles in their scabbards, but if we are attacked we shall fight to kill."

"Big words!" Muke-war-rah said scornfully. "Big words!"

"If Muke-war-rah doubts the fighting ability of the *to-e-titch-e,* he well knows how to test it." Those too were big words, but they had to be used, for if Muke-war-rah got the idea they were scared his braves would overwhelm the entire train.

"You are Tejano?"

"No," said Ross. "But we have learned many lessons from the Texans."

"You are Mejicano," Muke-war-rah insisted.

"I am not Mexican." He knew the Comanches' contempt for the Mexicans as fighters. He tapped his chest. "I am Godamme." The word was of Apache origin, taken from the familiar curse of the Americans, but it was known to most Southwestern tribes, and to all it meant the same: a hard-fighting, never-give-up white man, who, totally different from all Indians, retreated from no odds whatever.

Muke-war-rah grunted. The grunt might have meant anything or nothing. "You have plenty mules," he said. "I sell you this captive for ten mules."

Ross, to gain time, said, "I have seen no captive."

Muke-war-rah glanced at him again with his evil black eyes, and there was a sardonic light in them. "The Godamme think Muke-war-rah talks to throw his voice to the wind." He stood up suddenly, and Ross almost gasped. The Comanche was huge. He towered over the other Indians by a full head; he was even taller than Ross. He must have been six feet and a half, and had a torso like a barrel, legs like cottonwood logs.

"Santa María!" Muke-war-rah shouted, his eyes half-hooded.

A whimpering came from the tent behind him, and Ross realized the Comanche had a Mexican captive who must have repeated the phrase over and over as she prayed for deliverance. Ross began to harden himself for whatever was to appear.

"Santa María!" Muke-war-rah shouted.

The five Comanches sitting around the fire all looked toward the tent flap.

Muke-war-rah took two big steps and disappeared inside the tent. Suddenly he growled, and there were the sound of a great open hand against flesh, and a scream. Muke-warrah's Comanche phrases sounded vitupera-tive, and again Ross heard the slap, so hard it must almost have caved in the woman's cheekbone. Then Muke-war-rah appeared again in the door, dragging behind him, with no effort on his part, a Mexican woman. She was fighting, but he outweighed her three to one, and he literally dragged her to the fire. She continued to twist and turn, and tried to bite his hand, but once again the big hand swung against her face, and this time knocked her flat in the dust. She lay there, face down, perhaps momentarily unconscious.

"She is fight plenty hard." Muke-war-rah grinned. "Much spirit. You like."

Ross shrugged, pretending disinterest. He noted the many black marks on the woman's legs and arms and bare shoulders, and it was easy to see that she had been fighting steadily. It was also easy to guess that it had not done her any good, for the Comanches were not inhibited.

Ross shook his head as if to show his disinterest. "She does not belong to us."

"But do not all *to-e-titch-e* buy all other whites?"

"Perhaps—if they have the goods."

The woman was stirring. Muke-war-rah jabbed a heavy toe in her stomach. "You buy this one. I sell cheap. You take home and put in your teepee."

There were a lot of concepts among the Comanches that the Anglos or Mexicans didn't have, and that was one. "Her husband would buy her, but her husband is dead," Ross said at a guess.

"We know. We left him for the buzzards. And three children—too little—no good for work. We knocked their brains out on a rock."

165

The whimpering came again from inside, and Muke-war-rah nodded toward the tent. "That one is next if she does not work."

The woman on the ground was small and slender, and Ross saw that she was young.

"*¡Arriba!*" growled Muke-war-rah.

She got up slowly, and Ross heard Andrés gasp aloud. Her hair had not been combed since she had been captured, and her face, which had been pretty, was now a mass of purple bruises. Ross shuddered inwardly at what she had been through—the more so because he knew it had been of no avail, for a Comanche was stronger than any woman, and for the Comanches it was as simple as that.

She got on her knees and saw Ross and Andrés, and her eyes darted to Hermenijildo, still on horseback. She turned back quickly to Ross, a wild light of hope in her eyes. "You have come to rescue me?" she asked.

"*Señora,*" Ross said gently, "we have come to try." He did not dare tell her his limitations. "They out-number us considerably, and I do not know how we shall get along."

"He's a filthy beast!" She spat at Muke-war-rah sud-denly, and he slapped her again with his huge hand and sent her sprawling many feet away.

"For such a one," he said to Ross, "you would give much goods, hey?"

Ross watched the girl get up slowly. He tried to keep his feelings out of his face. "We might talk," he said carefully. "But if you injure her the price will go down."

She crawled to her hands and knees, with her black

hair over her eyes, her face swollen and miscolored, her eyes wild like the eyes of a trapped wolf. But there was a certain familiarity in her posture as she stared up at him that made him look closer.

"*Señora,*" he asked suddenly, "did you live on the Conchas?"

"*Sí, señor.*"

"Near Presidio?"

She nodded.

"In a small mud hut on the east bank?"

She nodded again.

"*Señora*"—his voice was as gentle as if he had been talking to a baby—"were you in Chihuahua thirty days ago?"

She nodded slowly.

"Your name is Carlota, and you picked up my hat from the street and gave it to me."

She stared at him.

"Your husband saved my life, *señora.* Now listen carefully: be patient and we shall try to get you free. It will not be easy but we shall keep trying. You must remember, *señora,* we will do the best we can. And don't give up hope, whatever happens."

She gazed at him a long time, trying to understand everything he meant. Finally she said, "*Espero, señor,*" but her voice sounded hopeless.

Andrés was staring at her with eyes wide in horror and pity. When Muke-wa-rah saw, his shrewd eyes grew calculating.

"Very nice, hey? *Simpática.* You give fifty mules, hey?"

Ross said quickly, "Your chief told me ten mules."

Muke-war-rah looked mockingly sad. "He has a bad memory. I said fifty mules, did I not?" he demanded of the five braves around the fire.

They nodded solemnly.

Ross took a deep breath. "The mules do not belong to us," he said.

Muke-war-rah shrugged. "If they are good mules, I do not care who owns them."

To change the subject, Ross asked, "Have you no more captives?"

"Not now," said Muke-war-rah. "We have more in another moon, when my braves get back from Mexico."

The brazenness of the Comanche was infuriating, but there was nothing Ross could do. He looked at Carlota, and tried to keep the compassion out of his face, because he knew if Muke-war-rah saw any sign of weakness he would be harder to deal with. "Have patience, *señora*," he said in a low voice. "We will do the best we can."

Muke-war-rah lifted her bodily from the ground by one arm and flung her through the tent opening. She tried hard to keep her feet, but went over head first with a force that shook the walls of the tent. Ross heard her breathing hard, trying not to sob.

Ross said, as casually as possible, "I will talk it over with the *teniente*. I cannot say what his decision will be."

Muke-war-rah said knowingly: "Who knows? She is a woman. My braves have all tried her and like her. Maybe one of them will give me sixty mules for her tomorrow."

Ross scoffed. "Your braves don't have sixty mules all put together."

Muke-war-rah only grinned scornfully.

Ross turned and took the reins of his black.

"I'll take thirty mules and that horse," said Muke-war-rah.

"I will talk it over," said Ross, and mounted.

Ish-a-ro-yeh said something to Muke-war-rah in Comanche.

Muke-war-rah's eyes widened. "One woman for a hundred men, hey?" A venal smile centered around his straight, cruel mouth. "I give you this woman for yours, Anglo."

Ross said harshly, "We do not trade women."

He led the way out of the camp, through the barking dogs, past eyes staring from tent flaps, Hermenijildo and Andrés followed silently. They passed the last teepee and walked their horses across the meadow and up the narrow path. At the top, Ross said: "Keep going until we get away from here. You never know when some brave is going to try for scalps."

When they got back, Tapia had no advice to offer, as Ross had anticipated. For there was none to offer. You paid the fifty mules and hoped for the best, or you went on and left the girl in Muke-war-rah's tent.

"We'll be short of mules," Ross said, "if we give up fifty."

"We can divide the burdens," said Apolinar. "My father will pay for the mules. I pledge it."

Ross shook his head. "We're barely started. We will not be able to buy mules anywhere until we get to

Arkansas. In the meantime, overloading the mules we have may be the difference between getting there with the bullion and being stranded out in the middle of the wilderness."

"We should have another wagon," said Hermenijildo.

"We haven't. Of course, a mule can transport a lot more in a wagon, but wagons can't go everywhere. It is better, not knowing the country, to pack the bullion in packsaddles. Then we won't have to leave any of it in a bed of quicksand or at the edge of a canyon that a wagon could not cross."

"Then—"

"Then," Ross said firmly, "we'll do it anyway. First thing in the morning we'll pick out fifty mules and go back. We'll redistribute the loads the best we can."

Hermenijildo looked grateful, Apolinar relieved, and Andrés joyful.

Andrés was up early, and Ross told him to get Soft-Shelled Turtle and to take three men besides Hermenijildo and Apolinar and ride slowly to the Comanche camp. They were to enter it and go to the tent of Muke-war-rah and wait at the fire, saying and doing absolutely nothing no matter what might happen in front of them. "Do you think you can do that, if her life depends on it?" asked Ross.

Andrés said gravely, "*Sí, señor,* I will do it."

"All right. Get going."

Then he took Plácido and spent considerable time looking over the mules and trying to pick out those with hidden faults that had developed on the drive. It required time, but at last they got the fifty mules, and Plácido and two of his *arrieros,* all armed, went along to drive the animals.

"I hope," said Ross, "to get it over with as soon as possible by sending the boys on ahead. That way we can dispense with some of the rigamarole."

As they drove the mules toward the west, Plácido said, "*Señor,* a party comes—fast. Several riders."

Ross watched. A faint spiral of dust hung in the early-morning air, and got bigger. He said, "Take the mules back. Warn Tapia."

"Plácido asked fearfully, "What do you think it is, *señor?*"

"I don't know," said Ross, watching, "but we'll soon find out."

He did. Andrés rode up at a furious gallop, foam hanging from his horse's mouth. "*¡Señor! ¡Señor!* The Comanches have gone! The tents are gone! Everything is gone!"

Chapter 14

For some reason the Comanches had taken fright and moved their camp during the night. There was no use chasing them, for even a huge band of Comanches could move faster than a hundred armed men; and even if a hundred armed men caught them—assuming the best of luck—they would be unable to attack them with any success. On occasion, a few determined men had done miraculous things against Indians, but only rarely, and never in the Indians' home territory or against the Indians and their families.

Ross was bitterly disappointed, but he told his lieutenants it was hopeless. The entire Southwest was infested with bands such as Muke-war-rah's, large and small, and all of them had captives sooner or later, and there were so many of them that nobody could do anything about it. The wilderness areas of Texas and New Mexico clear up to the Oregon line were controlled by the savages, with only here and there a group of whites forted up or a retaliatory expedition or a company of beaver trappers or miners to take a stand against them. The whites were a few hundreds at most, and there were many thousands of Indians; Ross forced himself to set his mind toward Arkansas.

Now began the long haul northeastward through the breaks below the Llano and across the bitter-salted rivers, past quicksand beds and over immense arid prairies. Here they were far beyond the frontier of Texas, for Austin was a long way east; they were no one knew how many hundreds of miles from Santa Fe, for to the north and west was only the impassable desert of the Llano, that vast expanse of table-flat prairie that few of them had ever seen.

They kept to the northeast and camped in pecan groves or mottes of oak and persimmon, and they fed well on buffalo meat—hump, tongue, and fat intestines—and Josefina spent her days, when they were not traveling, grinding corn in the *metate,* and her nights—Ross did not inquire.

The long miles stretched behind them, and the great

distances of Texas stretched ahead, and there never seemed to be an end to it. The Tonkawas identified the Brazos from its look and the taste of its water, and then demanded their pay—ten pounds of pressed tobacco— and disappeared, for now the caravan was in the heart of Comanche and Caygüa country, and any Tonkawa captured there was lucky to be roasted alive, for the Comanches claimed the Tonkawas cooked and ate Comanches and Caygüas. However that might be, it was distinctly poor judgment for any Tonkawa to go very far into this area; so Soft-Shelled Turtle and his silent companions faded into the vast wilderness and left the expedition to its own resources.

Ross had been watching the stars, and they turned their route a little to the north, thinking to avoid the Texan outposts, for now not only were they running the risk of creating an international dispute, but no one knew exactly what would happen if the Texans did find them. It was altogether possible that under the press of internal disturbances, the party in power might—even if they were disposed to wink at this "invasion" of Texas soil—be forced to take some defensive action, and this might end in confiscation of the bullion. Back in Chihuahua they had considered the possibility, but it hadn't seemed very important. Here it had reality, and so, having actually entered the republic and having traversed probably half of it, Ross had an additional worry on his mind.

It was important, therefore, to reach Indian Territory and travel down the north side of the Red River of Natchitoches. Confiscation was only something that *might* happen, of course, but with a third of a million dollars in bullion on the backs of the mules, Ross didn't want to take any chances.

The water got worse, and it became necessary to avoid the rivers and to find springs. Even some of the springs were impregnated with sulphur and gypsum and copper sulphate until the water was almost undrinkable. On a diet almost solely of buffalo meat, the men developed intermittent diarrhea, and Ross finally had Josefina steep great pots of tea from the inner bark of cottonwood trees. It was so bitter it was nauseating, but it stopped the diarrhea.

And so they continued day after day, winding their way along the buffalo trails, over the divides, down into the valleys, across the streams, up through the breaks and over the dry, endless prairies, until they came to a wide river of red water which they were unable to name. Tapia thought it might be the Red River; one of his dragoons said he had been on it and that it was the Brazos.

Ross pointed out that Soft-Shelled Turtle had already identified the Brazos, but Tapia reasoned that because Soft-Shelled Turtle had not felt comfortable in Comanche country, he had identified some other stream as the Brazos—perhaps the Colorado River of Texas—so as to get his pay and go back south. That was a reasonable supposition, and Ross decided they had better go north to be sure. The country was unmapped and they could identify it only by guess.

They crossed that river, which they now called the Brazos, in shallow water, for it was only the latter part of June, and lost only one mule in the quicksand. They threw a rope around the mule's neck and tried to pull it out with the horses, but because the mule fought furiously to get out it only enmired itself deeper. Ross sent for large branches to lay alongside the mule, and in the meantime cut the lashing and took off the packsaddle. The mule continued to struggle, and by the time the branches arrived there was nothing above the surface but its head, and it was impossible to save it. It brayed piteously until it went under.

They continued north, through a rather flat country of excellent grass, which began to put the mules in good shape. In occasional shallow breaks mesquite trees grew, and once in a while an isolated clump of small oak and blackjack trees.

They reached a shallow stream which they knew could not be the Red, and for the first time began to wonder if they had already crossed the Red. But Ross believed the only course was north, and they kept on, the prairie growing flatter and the grass more succulent. In some places it was as high as a mule's belly.

"We may hit the Arkansas," said Tapia one day. "I was on that river in 1828, when the governor of New Mexico sent an expedition to Bent's Fort."

Ross considered. "If we hit it, we'll come in a long way below Bent's Fort, I figure."

Three days later they stopped at the bank of a wide riverbed. There was hardly a foot of water in it, most of the bed being dry sand that was only a few feet below the surface of the prairie. The sides were sloping, so that access was easy. Ross rode into it and up and down the bed for a quarter of a mile each way, then came back and asked Tapia, "Do you think this is it?"

"It is difficult to say. It resembles it—but my memory is that the Arkansas had more water in it."

"Of course, this river, if it is the Arkansas, has come a long way—several hundred miles across the prairie. It might have dried up."

Tapia agreed, being plainly at a complete loss.

Plácido lined up the mules on the bank to let them drink, and Josefina almost immediately got out her *metate* and went to work.

Ross took Hermenijildo and rode across the river, watching the sand for signs of sinking. The surface of the sand, where it was dry, was soft like sand in the open desert; where it was wet it formed a compact sort of mat that quivered and gave under the weight of a horse and rider. But Ross was watching for any kind of sand where a horse's hoof would immediately sink in up to the fetlocks, and when he found such a spot he promptly wheeled the gelding and changed his course. He went into the muddy water to let the gelding drink, and he was sitting in the saddle wondering how much farther to go north when Hermenijildo said in a low voice, "Look up, *señor. ¡Los indios!*"

Ross jerked around and looked at the far bank. On a shelf of sand, not over fifty feet away, three Indians stood watching them. Ross's glance swept the country behind them for signs of others, but he saw nothing but a low semicircle of sandhills covered with thick green bushes now red with sandplums. Ross pulled up the gelding's head and rode straight across.

He made the sign for friend, and one of the Indians, black, slight, and seamed of face, though not old, asked, "You 'Merican?"

"American and Mexican," said Ross.

"I'm Si-ki-to-ma-ker—Black Beaver."

Ross smiled. After those long days through Texas, it was good to hear a name he knew. "Black Beaver, the Delaware?"

The Indian nodded. "Delaware. These my friends— Ni-co-man and Jim Linney."

Ni-co-man was a strange sight, for he had a large silver ring in his nose and wore a great turban, wrapped Turkish style, of brightly colored striped silk. Jim Linney, a well-known Delaware chief, was inconspicuous, wearing white man's pants without a belt, no shirt, and moccasins.

"What are you doing out here?" asked Ross.

"We came to hunt buffalo. No buffalo left yonder." He pointed east.

Ross got down and handed them each a sack of tobacco. They took it eagerly. "You know what river this is?"

"This," said Black Beaver, "Canadian River, all same South Canadian."

"You're sure it isn't the Arkansas?"

"No. Arkansas that way." He pointed north.

"Where's the Red River of Natchitoches?"

"That way." He pointed south.

Ross decided to test him. "Do you know where Santa Fe is?"

"Sure. Him that way." He pointed west. "One long

hike, by golly."

Ross laughed. "You've been a guide all over this country, haven't you?"

"Sure," said Black Beaver. "I no greenhorn."

"Well," said Ross, "I'm glad we met you."

Black Beaver nodded wisely. "Sure. You lost. You bad lost."

"We weren't sure how much farther to go."

"You been lost eight days now."

"What?"

"We watch. You no see. You too busy being lost. We come after."

Ross restrained a smile. "You know where New Orleans is?"

"Sure. Him that way." He pointed southeast. "Long way downriver."

Ross said, "I guess you've been everywhere."

"Sure," said Black Beaver. "I been California. Long way. Plenty sand."

"Your friends aren't saying much."

"Sure. They don't know much. I tell them, I talk, they keep still."

Ross grinned, and Black Beaver grinned back. "All right," Ross said. "We're lost. You're not. Will you guide us where we want to go?"

"You want to go to Arkansas," said Black Beaver.

Ross looked up. "How'd you know?"

Black Beaver raised his eyebrows. "Indian know more than white man think."

"Can you show us the way?"

"Sure. We guide. Two bits a day to Fort Towson."

"Two bits?"

"Two bits—all three." Black Beaver jabbed a fore-finger into each of his companion's chests and then into his own. "Two bits—all three. Cheap. Big bargain."

"We might want to go beyond Fort Towson."

"You no need guide for that. Any fool find way from Fort Towson."

"All right, you're hired."

"No tobacco," Black Beaver said. "No whisky."

"Most Indians want tobacco at least."

"We buy more tobacco with two bits than you give us. We not ignorant Indians. We learn white man's road. Get the money."

Ross squatted and began to draw a map in the sand. "You show me how to go."

"You pay first."

"Sure." Ross gave him a big silver Mexican dollar.

"Fine. Peso. Very good."

"I'll give you the rest at Fort Towson."

"Very good. I draw map."

He drew a crooked line that represented the river. He said, "You here. You lost. Fort Towson here." He made a cross mark two feet away. "Fort Towson not lost."

"All right." Ross stood up. "How far?"

Black Beaver squinted as he counted up. "Two weeks. Not bad unless rain. If rain, very bad. Three weeks. You better off go home."

"In this case," said Ross, "we go ahead even if it rains every day."

Black Beaver nodded. "Sound like damn'-fool white man. Where you come from?"

"Mexico."

"All right. Get mules across. We start out."

They took the wagons across first. The wagons were considerably lighter than they had been at the start, and easier to handle. The long train of mules was well trail broken, and each animal followed another, even across the river.

They followed the river east on its left bank, and Black Beaver showed them where to take short cuts that saved miles, and always brought them up to fresh water.

They had a week under bright, sunny skies. Then it rained, and the prairie was a sea of mud. Black Beaver advised waiting a few days, for it took twelve mules to pull a wagon, and the wheels after a hundred yards were monstrous things covered with hundreds of pounds of sticky mud.

Ross agreed to wait. The skies cleared and turned to a turquoise blue dome; the grass came out emerald-green on the long slopes, and in twenty-four hours the sun and wind had dried out the gumbo until it was firm footing, and they went ahead.

They pulled into Fort Towson early one afternoon, with the June sun steaming on the mud flats down near the river, buzzards circling the sky, coyotes watching from the hilltops, and quail running before them and occasionally bursting into a feathered bombshell of flight that caused considerable trouble among the mules.

The fort was composed of many buildings, all of hewn logs, neatly constructed, with brick chimneys, and with porches at the front of each building. All were whitewashed, and there were separate buildings outside the fort itself for blacksmith's shop, bakery, store, stables, quarters for the laundresses and camp women. And everywhere there were pleasant gardens.

They drew up on the last hill and sat their horses for a moment and looked at it. "The first time in two months," said Ross, "that we have seen anything resembling civilization."

"This her," said Black Beaver. "You owe us fifteen days—$3.75. You give one dollar already."

"Very good," Ross said. He counted out three pesos. "I'll pay you one extra day for being truthful."

"You no have to pay for that," Black Beaver said. "Only bad Indians tell untruth. But we happy get two bits anyway. Thank you."

Ross left the train of wagons and mules on the slope to avoid overrunning the grounds and went directly to the building which boasted an American flag. As he passed the guardhouse, he saw, standing on a barrel head before it, a young soldier with an empty bottle in each hand and a board hung from his neck marked "Whisky Seller." He told them where to find the commander.

Ross found Major Fauntleroy and reported the cargo. The major said he saw no reason why he couldn't go right ahead, there being no regulations against importation of bullion; in fact, he thought, the United States would be right glad to get ten thousand pounds of gold and silver.

He asked, "Are you with Connelly's expedition?"

"Yes, sir."

"Dr. Connelly got into Pecan Point, down the river a few miles, about a week ago, expecting you, sir."

"Maybe you can tell me where I am, exactly."

"Look at this map. Here's Fort Towson, on the Kiamichi River, surrounded by more Choctaw doggeries than you can shake a stick at."

"Doggeries?"

"Cheap saloons. The soldiers can't buy whisky on the grounds, so the Indians set up these doggeries just outside the reservation. Now, then, Doaksville is right here, about a mile from us; that's the capital, so-called, of the Choctaw Nation; big agency there. We're only a couple of miles from the Red."

"The Red River of Natchitoches?"

"Yes, sir. Just below where the Kiamichi runs into the Red is Jonesboro, and just below that is Pecan Point. There's an inn at Pecan Point; that's why Dr. Connelly stayed there."

"That brings up a question: What can I do with my men? I've got about a hundred men and one woman, and they'll be tired of camping out. I've got to do something with them while I go to New Orleans."

"A woman, eh? No trouble there. Women are scarce as hen's teeth out here. But the men." The bewhiskered major shook his head. "There's a problem, I declare. I reckon the best is to scatter 'em up and down the river; the Indians will be glad to put them up for a price; it won't be fancy but it'll be cheap. Some of the people at Doaksville will take in boarders."

"Sounds all right for the men. How about the mules?"

"How many mules?"

"Seven hundred, less twenty-two."

"Hit the quicksand?"

"They drank in the Pecos."

"I heard it was like that. Well, I'd guess you better see Black Beaver. He'll either—"

"The Delaware?"

"Yes. Know him, I see. He'll either pasture 'em for you or put 'em out to pasture with the Choctaws. Absolutely honest; you'll get every head back in fine shape. Never worry about Black Beaver."

"For how much?"

"Oh, say five cents a month per head. Something like that."

He went outside and stood on the porch. His wagons were up on the slope, and his great band of mules was spreading out, some grazing, some lying down with their packs on. All over the grounds of the fort, men in blue uniforms were making their way toward the train. Some were already there, and half a dozen were gathered around Josefina.

Ross stretched. It was wonderful to have arrived. "Pretty soon," he told Hermenijildo, "we'll have a hot bath and sleep in a real bed—maybe even a feather bed."

"I haven't seen my wife in a long time," said Hermenijildo.

"A few more months," said Ross, "and you'll be home. Maybe you'll have a *niño* by that time."

"Oh, no, *señor,* we won't be gone that long, I'm sure."

"No, I suppose not," Ross said absently. "If we can

183

get our goods at New Orleans and run them back up the river, we should be able to start back right away."

"If this were Mexico," said Hermenijildo, "I would be very skeptical, but this is the United States, and you always do things with great speed, and there are not the innumerable delays that one can encounter in Mexico, when nothing moves and nothing happens."

Ross said: "You sound gloomy. You aren't predicting anything, are you?"

Hermenijildo said, "I don't know, *señor.* It is a feeling I have."

Chapter 15

Connelly rode in the next day on a big Missouri mule, and Ross heard his roar a quarter of a mile away: "Ross Phillips, where are you?"

Ross was in the officers' cabin which had been lent to him and the three young Mexicans and Tapia. He went out as Connelly flung himself from the mule and ran to meet him. Connelly was a bearish man, big, strong, quick. He put an arm around Ross and said, "Fine beard you've got, my boy; wish my hair was brown like yours."

The next morning they went to look for the men. Most of them had hangovers; some were still drunk; two were in bed with Indian women, seven were in jail for fighting in the doggeries around Fort Towson, but in no case had anyone been seriously hurt. Ross and Connelly established credit for them at the post and then sat down over a bottle of New Orleans rum, along with Hermenijildo and Apolinar, to discuss the next move.

"Where's Andrés?" asked Connelly.

Apolinar said apologetically, "He's very fond of the girl."

"What girl?" asked Ross, but he knew the answer as soon as he asked.

"Josefina."

"Where's Plácido, then?"

"He went off with an Indian girl."

"Who is Josefina?" Connelly asked, puzzled.

Ross shook his head wearily. "Don't ask me to explain the entire situation or we'll be sitting here all night, but the fact remains that this is Josefina of the Nine Cats, of whom I'm sure—"

Connelly groaned. "*¡Caramba!* It is one thing to take Andrés away from his father's *rancho,* but to allow him to get serious over that little *chingada*—"

Ross said: "We will have to rely on Apolinar and Hermenijildo to look out for him in any event. Meanwhile, we have many serious things to do. We must try to keep our men together and out of trouble as much as possible. We also have to buy seventy wagons and another hundred mules, and we have to look toward hiring 150 more men."

"Why so many men?" asked Major Fauntleroy.

"We brought out," said Connelly, "about ten thousand pounds of bullion on muleback, and that did not require many men. But the trip back we'll have about three hundred thousand pounds of merchandise—about an even trade, pounds for dollars—and we'll have to have a lot of wagons because the goods will be bulky. This also requires more men, for wagons need upkeep."

"You'll have to move fast to cross Texas before the northers come down. That will be any time from November first on." He looked at them. "Your biggest trouble will be wagons. The Texans have been buying all they could get, and there aren't enough wagons for sale this side of Pittsburgh." He leaned back and tossed down his rum. "I wouldn't count on spending Christmas in Chihuahua, gentlemen."

Hermenijildo's face was long. "Not—by Christmas?" he asked.

Ross said glumly, "Not until next summer—if the major has it figured right—because we won't be able to leave after October first on account of the grass. We'll be forced to wait here until next April."

Hermenijildo gulped down his rum and stared at the table.

"His wife is *preñada,*" Ross explained. "It's his first one."

"Oh!" Connelly said. "That's easy fixed. You'll go back on the boat with me. We'll be in Chihuahua by the first of October."

Hermenijildo looked up. "No, *señor,*" he said quietly. "I have started this trip and I will finish it if God is willing. I shall miss my Chonita if I am forced to stay in this awful country—forgive me, Major—"

"Don't mind me," said Fauntleroy, pouring more rum. "I've said much worse myself."

Hermenijildo was silent for a moment. "But I am staying until the end," he announced, and Ross knew there was no point in arguing with him. . . .

Recruiting men, they visited all the saloons in the adjoining area of Texas, across the Red River. Ross went to all those in the immediate vicinity in Arkansas, and then began on the doggeries around the fort. On the second night, he and Connelly went into a doggery about four miles east of Towson—a half-dugout, half-mud hut, with no windows, and a dirt floor. Beside a dead fireplace in one wall, two rough-hewn planks were laid on empty cracker hogsheads. A soldier, half-drunk, stood uncertainly at the crude bar; half a dozen men in buckskin and rough home-made clothing sat on the dirty floor, drinking; the bartender was an unshaved, dirty, fattish man who looked like a Choctaw half-breed. Through all the sour stench of bodies, his beady eyes looked them over, and he waited, saying nothing.

Ross dropped a silver peso on the plank. "Whisky," he said.

The bartender turned to a small keg and held a dirty glass under the spigot. He set it down in front of Ross and filled another. He took the peso, examined it, and gave back four *reales* change. Ross put the money in the wallet inside his buckskin shirt, lifted the glass and looked at Connelly. "Here's to love," he said in Spanish, "and death and taxes. Let's hope there's enough alcohol in this stuff to kill germs."

"I doubt it," Connelly said sourly, also in Spanish. He raised the glass. "This stuff is made in a hog trough, out of lye water, with tobacco for color and a bottle of cherry brandy for flavor."

The bartender said harshly, "We don't cotton to folks talkin' foreign in here."

Ross's hand froze in mid-air. "Then why is the man in the corner talking French?" he demanded, suddenly aware of the hostility of the bartender.

"Hey!" said the man with the red stocking cap. "Somebody call my name?" He got up, towering to the very top of the doggery. In fact, he bent his neck to keep his head from bumping on the ceiling. He took two steps toward Ross. "You speak about me?" His eyes blazed wider as Ross declined to answer. He grabbed Ross's buckskin shirtfront with a huge hand. "You!" he roared.

Ross didn't hesitate. He knew they had been primed for him. Trusting Connelly to take care of the bartender, he threw the whisky in the Frenchman's eyes and bored into his stomach with both fists, packing all the hard brawn of ten years on the trail into the blows.

The big man gave ground, gasping and sputtering. But in a moment he was back, reaching with huge arms to pull Ross to him in a bearhug. Ross whirled as the big hands caught him. He got his back to the Frenchman, grabbed one of the big arms, and pulled the Frenchman over his shoulder and bounced him hard on his back on the dirt floor. Instantly Ross pinned both big arms and straddled the man's head, with one knee in the hollow of each shoulder. After glancing up to see Connelly holding a six-shooter on the bartender and the onlookers, he made his thumbs rigid and said, "You want to fight, *cochon?*"

The big man looked up, saw the thumbs aimed at his eyes, and turned pale. "No!" he said. "I am only giving you the test: They have say you are one tough man from Chihuahua, and I am having a leetle fun! No, *m'sieu'*, I no want fight!"

Ross let him up. They left the doggery.

"A strange thing," Connelly said a moment later. "They were all set for us. The whole thing was deliberate."

Ross agreed. "The Frenchman was planted there to whip me and make us lose face with men who might sign up for the trip back."

"It sounds like Cordero's work," said Connelly.

Connelly and Ross took the gold downriver to New Orleans and got a receipt from the bank. Ross's father was in Baltimore. Connelly got a letter of credit for $342,055. He and Ross had a couple of drinks at Hewlett's Exchange, and Connelly felt pretty good. "We've made 10 per cent on our specie already, and a fat profit on the bullion." He slapped Ross on the shoulder. "Thanks to you for getting the train through."

Ross said lightly, "We still have to get back."

"I anticipate no trouble," said Connelly. "As soon as I leave New Orleans I'm going straight to Presidio del Norte and be sure Don Lawreano is kept in a good humor until you get there."

"You ought to take Josefina with you, then."

"Not me," said Connelly. "That woman scares the hell out of me. D'you suppose I'm getting old?"

"Hard to say. I suppose you've bought the goods already."

"Matter of fact, no. I ran into so many questions trying to buy the wagons I decided I'd better keep my mouth shut and take my chances. If I go around town spending a third of a million dollars for goods, the Mexican consul will hear about it sooner or later—and I want to be out of town when he does."

"He'll report it anyway, won't he?"

"Yes, but he'll take his time. It may be six months or a year. By that time we'll be on our second or third expedition."

"Where do we go to buy the goods?"

"Pierre's. He has more stock than anybody."

"Why don't we get there, then?"

Pierre's was run by a Yankee storekeeper named Wilkins, who looked at them over his nose glasses and said in a nasal voice, "Be you the fellers came through Texas with seven hundred mules?"

"We be," said Ross.

"Wall, I reckon you're after goods to take back."

"That we are," said Connelly.

"We got a right smart stock here, but if what I heerd is true we won't be able to fill your list completely. Got a boat comin' in from Baltimore next week, though."

"Let's see how far we can go," said Connelly.

He started first on the list of food for the return trip, and Wilkins was able to fill it completely. Then he began to enumerate the trade goods he wanted: "Ten thousand bolts of colored calico and gingham; fifteen hundred alarm clocks; fifty thousand packs of needles—"

The storekeeper's mouth was hanging open. "Mister, you won't find that much goods in all of New Orleans. You got the money to pay for it?" he asked suddenly.

Connelly said, exasperated: "There's a third of a million dollars in the Merchants' Bank. Do you want to do business with us?"

The old man swallowed audibly. "I sure do," he said finally. "I—well—I never seen any kind of order like that." He recovered. "All right, mister—Dr.—Connelly, let's take that there list one thing at a time and I'll mark down what I've got and what's coming in by boat, and I think we'll have you fixed up in a few days." He was all business. "This here could be a right smart thing for New Orleans, to get this trade going—where'd you say you're from?"

"Chihuahua," said Ross.

The old man scratched his face. "Chihuahua? I heerd of it, I reckon. Seems to me I know somebody went to Chihuahua some years back. Name of—"

"Jennison?"

"Not him. No. Lemme see. Manderson? Mangum! That's it! Mangum! Young feller, like."

"Mangum?" repeated Ross. "Ed Mangum?"

"Sure. Ed Mangum. Knowed him when he was a little feller."

"Friend of yours?"

"Lemme see now. Let's start with needles. No, not a friend, exactly. Used to come in my store up in New Hampshire. Funny child, now. How many needles you say? I've got some cartons in the attic. I'll look for them later, because there'll be more stuff to check up there."

"What about Mangum?" asked Ross.

Wilkins looked at him over his glasses. "Peculiar sort of fellow. Even ten years old he was sort of stiff-necked. Always pretended to look down on things back

191

home. Always talkin' about Paris or Constantinople—always pretendin' to be something he never was."

"He hasn't changed much," Connelly observed.

"Nope. Didn't reckon he would. The feller didn't get on so good at home, and I always figgered he wanted to go to some foreign country, figgerin' he'd have a better chance."

"Or figuring," said Connelly, "that going to a distant place would set him apart from everybody else."

"Yep, guess you're right. He did that. Never heard how he come out."

"He's still trying," said Ross.

"Shoulda been satisfied at home. Had a nice family, good raisin'. Now let's have a look at print goods. That's in the back, here."

After a week of buying, Connelly was elated. He had used the storekeepers to beat down prices, even in the face of shortage, for all wanted to get in on the Chihuahua trade, and as a result he had an enormous quantity of goods to take back to Chihuahua. "It damn' near staggers me," he told Ross. "We never hauled any loads like that from Independence."

They stopped for a drink. "There's only one thing bothering me now," said Ross, looking at Connelly across the round table. "We'll get to Pecan Point, all right, but what if we get stuck with all this stuff in Presidio?"

Connelly laughed. "Don't let it worry you. That's my job—and with Irigoyen on our side we'll have no trouble." He leaned over. "Do you have any idea how

192

much we can turn this load of goods for?"

"How much?" asked Ross.

"This will stagger you," said Connelly. "We'll clear at least a million dollars on this deal."

Ross looked at him. "My share would be two hundred thousand," he said thoughtfully.

He told Connelly good-bye three days later and swung aboard the riverboat *Rover* with his carpetbag. Valeria was on his mind more strongly than ever, and he found himself constantly translating his share of the profit into land and horses or land and cattle.

He reached Pecan Point and rented storage space for the goods.

Santiago had been in jail three times for fighting. One of Tapia's men killed an American soldier, and there was a to-do with the Mexican consul in New Orleans. The Mexican teamsters and *arrieros* got into fights with the Choctaws over their women. A Choctaw was killed, and an *arriero* was charged with murder. A teamster was killed and a Choctaw girl was charged with murder.

Ross called a conference of Tapia and his three assistants, but Andrés did not appear. "Where is he?" asked Ross.

"He's rented a house over in Arkansas and is living there with Josefina," said Hermenijildo.

"What does Plácido say about it?"

"He grins," said Tapia, "and says she will come back to him."

Ross said anxiously, "Is he talking of getting married?"

"He's tried already," said Apolinar, "but the priest

won't marry them because Josefina is not paid up with the church."

Ross felt a little relief. He pulled the cork out of a bottle of rum. "We've got trouble on our hands, *hombres*. As you observe, we have goods, but mighty few wagons."

"Ten so far," said Hermenijildo.

Ross poured a drink for each. "That leaves us sixty short. How you coming with the mules, Apolinar?"

"I've bought eighty-two," said Apolinar. "The prices have been high, but—" He shrugged.

"Never mind the prices. Get the mules. We can't pull those wagons ourselves." Ross turned to Hermenijildo. "How about teamsters?"

Hermenijildo shook his head. "The luck is very bad, *señor*. I have engaged eighteen so far."

Ross frowned. "Why is this?"

Hermenijildo was thoughtful. "It is hard to say, *señor*. I have made the rounds of the saloons and public places in this area, and—I don't know." He shook his head. "They ask strange questions, and they make insinuations. They say that this is a war party for the Mexican Government, and that we are heading into a trap, and the Texans will annihilate us."

"Also," said Apolinar, "they say we will not pay them—that we will turn them over to the Comanches just before we get there to avoid paying."

Ross thought about it. "Has anybody heard about any stranger in the country lately?"

They all shook their heads but Tapia. "*Señor*. I recall a big man who has gotten into fights several times. He

194

is a man of one eye and one ear."

"Link Habersham!" Ross exclaimed.

"You know him?" asked Fauntleroy.

Ross nodded slowly.

"He's a bad *hombre*," Tapia said soberly.

Ross nodded. "I'll start looking for him tonight. Hermenijildo, you and Apolinar want to come along to make it a fair fight?"

Both nodded eagerly.

"Very well. As soon as supper is over. And you'd both better drink a pint of olive oil if you have any intention of drinking the poison they serve in the doggeries."

"*Sí, señor.*"

They did not find Habersham that night, although they encountered indications that he had been there.

A number of delays began to plague Ross. He waited for nine long weeks, from the nineteenth of August to the twenty-first of October. It rained almost every day, and it rained hard. Occasionally in the afternoon the sun would come through for a few hours, but the next morning the rain would be pelting down again. He rode out on the black gelding to look at the country, and found it a quagmire of sticky mud. The old Indians said there had never been anything like it; but that was small comfort.

Thirty-six wagons came up from New Orleans through Natchitoches, and fourteen came from St. Louis up the Arkansas through Van Buren, which was the nearest regular stop for freight and mail. They had almost enough mules, but now, Ross noted wryly, nothing to do but feed them until spring. He notified all teamsters the expedition would not leave until about April first. Some of the Mexican skinners found work around the fort and on freighter lines from Van Buren and Fort Smith to agencies in the Indian Country.

Ross suggested Hermenijildo go home to be with Chonita, but the young man refused, saying he was going to go through with it all the way. Apolinar was very popular with the unmarried daughters of officers at the fort. Andrés came in once a week to visit, and professed himself quite happy with Josefina.

By the first of December the rains had stopped and the ground was reported firm in all directions, but by that time the grass was gone and the mules would have no forage along the way.

In January the rest of the wagons arrived. In February Black Beaver went to St. Louis to accompany a party of surveyors going to the western reaches of Kansas country. In March, Ross called in Tapia and his three assistants. He was a little shocked at the appearance of Andrés; the young man had grown fat and rather greasy-looking and not too clean. But Ross outlined plans for gathering their men. He told Andrés to check over every wagon and grease every axle, and he made a mental note to double-check behind him, for Andrés did not appear to be the same man he had been on the way northeast.

Ross assigned Apolinar to find Indian guides, reminding him that on the return trip they would follow the south side of the Red River, in territory unknown to them, until they hit their trail of the previous summer. They would be going through territory inhabited by dif-

ferent tribes: Cherokees, Wacoes, Caddoes, Wichitas—
and it was desirable to have guides familiar with the terrain and the natives.

For himself Ross reserved what he anticipated
would be the hardest task; that of gathering a crew to
drive seventy wagons and seven hundred pack mules.
He rode the gelding to Van Buren, accompanied by
Hermenijildo, but it was a silent journey. It was March
and still too early for the dogwood to show its gorgeous
blossoms, but the first pale green shoots of grass were
breaking through the matted carpet of the prairie; following the protracted rain of the previous fall, the grass
would undoubtedly be plentiful.

Ross wondered about Valeria. The winter, in some
ways slow, had gone too fast in others. And even
assuming great leisureliness in Mangum's suit, Ross
faced the fact that almost a year had gone by and he had
not spoken his mind. As he watched the buds forming
on the dogwood, he realized it had been spring in Chihuahua when they had left.

A year had elapsed; and while a year on the road
might seem short, a year in Chihuahua might seem very
long.

Chapter 16

He and Hermenijildo went into the Freighters'
Saloon at Van Buren. "It may not be very good
whisky," said Ross, "but at least it's whisky."
"Are you Ross Phillips?" asked a nasal voice.

Ross looked up. The first thing he saw was a nickel-plated star, and above it a thin face with long, drooping mustaches. "I'm Phillips," he said.

The man held out a paper. "I'm Tallman, deputy sheriff. Got a summons for you."

"For what?"

"Murder."

Ross laughed. "You're joking."

"No joke, mister. You killed a man named Kerlérec in April last year."

Ross stared at him. "That was in Chihuahua—and it wasn't murder. It was self-defense."

"I ain't the judge, mister."

"What do you propose to do?"

"Put you in jail."

Ross got up, now taut. "You think you can take me?"

"I don't know about that, mister. I'm nearin' sixty and I admit I ain't the fighter I was once. But if I can't, somebody else will, because this is the law you're talkin' to, mister—not John Tallman."

Ross said, "Very well, if you represent the law—you haven't got a corpus delicti, have you?"

"How?"

"There's no body."

"There's one in Chihuahua."

"How do you know? Did you see it?"

The lawman scratched his head. "Well, now—"

Ross said: "Mister, we're establishing a trade route that can mean a lot to Arkansas. I'm up here right now to hire men. Why don't you go ask the judge about that corpus delicti?"

"I mought do that—but you better be here when I get back."

Ross nodded, but as soon as Tallman got outside he led Hermenijildo through the back door. "They'd take years to get extradition papers through from Mexico—if there is such a thing," he said, "but if we've run afoul of Kerlérec's friends it won't make any difference. The weather's better at Fort Towson anyway."

On Saturday afternoon he began to make the rounds. It was a beautiful spring day in Indian Territory; the sky was deep blue and cloudless; the grass had begun to give the hills an emerald green look that meant good grazing. A hawk floated in the sky, and the good earthy smell of growing things in moist, rich soil made a man want to run and stretch his legs with the colts on the hillside.

But within the dank dimness of the Choctaw doggeries all was dark and brooding, and the only looks Ross got were scowls. He was openly contemptuous of their liquor. He ordered it, paid for it, and let it stay on the boards. "They're sinkholes," he told Hermenijildo, "and since they're determined to be antagonistic to us anyway, I'd as soon give them good reason to be. It will spread our fame faster."

In each place he announced verbally that he wanted competent teamsters for the trip to Chihuahua; he would start within the week, and wages would start as each man signed up.

He got no takers. No one even made inquiry—and by this he knew they had been primed, and were only waiting for the explosion.

It came about ten o'clock Saturday night. It had been dark for two hours, and the night sounds of bullbats and owls and coyotes singing on the hilltops were harbingers of peace and tranquillity, but in the foul depths of the candle-lighted doggeries, saturated with the fumes of turpentine lamps, the rank smell of tobacco, and the sour sweat of unbathed bodies, there was no such indication.

The explosion came in an unusually big place known as Choctaw Tom's. Ross and Hermenijildo and Apolinar descended the dirt steps and walked out into the low room. Without looking around, Ross ordered whisky for the three. He paid for it and let it sit, turned his back to the boards that formed a counter, and made his announcement in a loud voice.

For the first time that night he got a response. From a group of men sitting on the floor at the end of the room he heard a voice:

"How are you payin'?"

"Twenty-five dollars a month and found."

"How do we know we'll get it?"

"How do you know you'll need it?" answered Ross. "You may die of a weak heart before you get there."

Silence. No rumble of approval at this sally. No sound whatever—and Ross knew it was coming. He said to Hermenijildo, "The knife! ¡*Pronto!*"

He felt the handle, and took hold of it, turning it within his fingers, behind his back, waiting for the next question.

"They say you're wanted in Arkansas for killing a man."

"They say many things," Ross answered. "I may be wanted again." He took a step forward. "There may be a reward on my head for all I know. Do you want to claim it?"

"I'll claim it!" said a heavy voice, and Link Habersham sprang to his feet. His head almost touched the sod ceiling, and he came forward on bent knees, a bowie knife in his right hand.

Ross took a step into the open. "Twice we've met," he said, "and you've lost an eye and an ear. What have you put up now?"

Habersham growled. He was a ghoulish sight without one ear and with one eye closed, but the open eye burned with a furious fever that could be quenched only by blood.

Ross said aloud, "My friends will shoot any who interfere," and heard the sound of weapons drawn from leather holsters.

Habersham said, "I thought it would be a fair fight."

"It will be fair," said Ross, "if we have to kill all your friends to make it so." He said to Hermenijildo, "Get that bartender out from behind the counter."

Hermenijildo said sharply, "Move! *¡Pronto!*" and Ross heard the bartender's shuffling feet.

He looked beyond the circling Habersham and saw the beetle-browed, scowling faces of Indians, Negroes, whites, and half-breeds, and knew their sympathies—such as they were—were with Habersham, perhaps because Habersham had plied them with rotgut on Cordero's money. Ross turned on one heel, feet apart but well under him.

Habersham was moving from side to side, keeping his distance, waiting for an opening, the blade of his big fourteen-inch knife held low before him.

Ross tried to keep his back in the general direction of the camphene lamp, whose yellow flame made Habersham's dirty skin look scrofulous.

Habersham lunged to Ross's left. Ross, remembering the man's trick in Chihuahua, sidestepped but did not attempt to follow up, standing poised, his knife at the level of his waist. It was well he refrained, for Habersham, seeming about to plunge head first into the counter, suddenly whirled in his tracks and chopped hard with his knife at about the height of a man's kidneys.

Ross grinned.

Habersham backed away, now thoroughly aroused. He began to move to the left, and as he faced the light squarely, Ross moved in suddenly and slashed at his neck.

But Habersham had anticipated the move. He ducked to one side, and, like Ross, stood for an instant waiting to see what Ross would do.

Ross, too, had control of his movements, and he stopped short to meet the expected thrust. But Habersham backed away.

Ross now was sweating freely, and that was a good sign, for it meant loosened muscles. For a few seconds he heard the harsh breathing of the men in the room, and a spat as somebody propelled tobacco juice into a corner.

Habersham too was sweating and moving easily. His one eye glared with hatred, but that was the only sign of emotion about him. He had dropped his hat as he came out, and his uncombed hair, soiled and matted, showed spots of gray. He wasn't over thirty-five, but he had been long on the Trail—long enough to feel no compunction.

Ross was now facing the light, while Habersham maneuvered to get it directly behind him. Ross moved, and Habersham growled and rushed straight forward, for a moment tired of fencing and wanting to close.

Ross jumped the other way and was tempted to take a cut at the man but again refrained, and again discovered it had been wise, for Habersham turned just when it seemed he was off balance.

But as Link regained his stance, Ross leaped in, sliced once, backed, and sliced again. He saw the big blade flash in the yellow light, and strained against it with his left arm. His own knife felt the drag of flesh as he drew it back, and then he was beyond Habersham's reach. His knife blade dripped, and Habersham's left arm and shoulder showed blood that looked black in the camphene light.

Habersham roared and rushed. Ross met him full on. They strained against each other. Ross bowed his back against the greater leverage of Habersham, and felt the man give. He pushed hard, and the man fell backward, seeming to be off balance. Ross was on him like an eagle on a rabbit. Habersham had his left forearm over his face to guard his throat, but Ross tried to get through.

Then he felt Habersham's legs gather under him as Link threw him off, stabbing with the knife at the same time. Ross felt the blade go between two ribs, but not deeply. Hurled through the air by the force of Habersham's leg thrust, he knew he had been fooled again.

Habersham, on his feet, kicked the knife out of Ross's hand and stabbed him through the left shoulder. Ross saw black for a moment, and then Habersham was sitting on his stomach, his back toward Ross's head.

Ross, weakening from the two stab wounds, felt the point of the knife as Habersham sliced the rawhide thong that laced up his trousers. He realized with horror what was about to happen. With a furious effort, he threw himself up, seized Habersham's head in both hands, and twisted the man to the floor. He smothered the knife by wrestling Habersham over and over on the dirt floor, until he could reach his own knife, which lay against one of the kegs that held the counter. He snatched it up, then drove it deep into Habersham's jugular vein.

He got to his feet, breathing hard, and looked at the scowling faces around him. "Anybody—wants to go to Chihuahua—see me—at the fort," he said.

The night air smelled good, and he took in great gulps of it. He gave the knife back to Hermenijildo. "I'm getting old," he said, "when I can't go through a knife fight without breathing like a wind-broken stallion."

"It was a magnificent battle," Apolinar said in awe.

Chapter 17

Men began to drift in the next day, and by Sunday night Ross had engaged 141.

Josefina rode in on a mule that evening, and Ross was relieved, in a way, to see that she showed no apparent change. He had expected some such degeneration as had occurred in Andrés, but Josefina looked exactly the same—no older, no wiser, no different. Ross had had it in mind to refuse to allow her to go back with the expedition, but he considered Andrés, and changed his opinion. Whatever else happened—and regardless of the change already made in Andrés—Ross considered it his inescapable duty to deliver him back to Chihuahua.

He said to Josefina, "*Señora,* you will understand that you will have to grind corn to pay your way?"

She looked at him with black eyes that seemed to contain a kind of primitive wisdom, and said, meekly, "*Por supuesto, señor*—of course," without taking notice of her change of status in his eyes as shown by his addressing her as *señora.*

He was not able to hire Indian guides, for Habersham had spread a great deal of talk about the Cherokees in northeast Texas being on the warpath as a result of Lamar's expulsion order, and no Indian wanted to be caught in Texas guiding a party of whites.

And so in April, 1840, almost exactly a year from the time they had left Chihuahua, the great caravan of 70 wagons, 850 mules, and 225 men left Fort Towson with 380,000 pounds of trade goods for Chihuahua. In spite of the long delay, the prospects were still bright. The vast quantity of goods had been well preserved, and since it had been bought originally with an eye to time spent on the trail, there was no loss except for a few packets of rusted needles. The cotton goods had been aired and exposed to the sun as much as possible, and there was little or no mildew.

All in all, Ross thought, as he sat the black gelding and watched the long, long line of wagons and mules follow the Kiamichi south toward the Red, they had come through the winter in remarkably good shape, and no harm had been done except delay. The cargo still represented a great fortune, and his share would be substantial. The unanticipated expense in connection with the long layover would be absorbed easily by the high prices always current in Chihuahua.

He shook hands with Fauntleroy and younger officers of the fort, wheeled the gelding, and galloped after the train. Andrés was still in charge of the wagons. Plácido had a mule of his own to ride.

Ross had hired a guide from near Pecan Point to show them the way across the Red, for the river, spread out over the valley by the backing up from the Great Raft, was several miles wide and looked like a vast morass of swamp, with islands of rank vegetation, pools of still brown water; somewhere, underneath matted entanglements of logs that had themselves become floating islands, flowed the live current of the river—not always following the path cleared by Henry Shreve a few years before.

It required three days for the big caravan to ford the river, and then once again they were on firm ground and the long expedition set its face to the southwest. They rounded the great bend of the Red and turned due west. The sun was warm and bright, and Ross felt invigorated and optimistic for a fast trip. Then it rained.

For weeks they fought the sticky mud, hitching twenty mules onto a wagon and taking them forward a few at a time. The Red rose and overspread its banks, and they were lost in a sea of mud and water and almost impassable fallen timber and brush.

They seldom saw the sun. The leaden skies dripped water incessantly; the stars at night were hidden by clouds. For days at a time they were not sure of their directions, but Ross drove the train forward blindly, relentlessly, every morning hoping for a break, and every night, though exhausted and beaten by the prodigious efforts required to move the train even three miles through the sticky mud, he chafed at the seeming conspiracy of Nature to hold them back.

During the second week they had a rash of squealing axles, and Ross rode back one day to find Andrés.

"We'll never get these wagons across the Pecos without grease on the axles," he said sternly.

Andrés looked up, his formerly neat black mustache now scraggly, and looking somehow in keeping with his fat face. "It might be that I missed some," he admitted.

Ross said sharply: "I have been examining the wheels of every wagon now for some days. There are no fresh finger marks on the spokes."

"I have not felt good," said Andrés.

Ross looked at him, disgusted. With some men it was like that; give them a woman who wanted nothing better than to lie on her back, and you had a man with no ambition but to accommodate her. With some it was different: a willing woman made them want to work the harder—but with Andrés, no.

Ross got back to the subject of wagons. "This will have to be taken care of, Andrés. We'll never move this train to Chihuahua without every man doing his job, and I expect you to do yours."

Andrés mumbled, "*Sí, señor*," and Ross rode off, not at all satisfied but still hopeful.

The rain lifted and the mud dried out. They had two good days, and then they hit the Cross Timbers. Again they were cruelly punished by the lack of guides. Ross rode to the north and forded the river but found no break. He rode a day's journey south and found no break, and there was nothing to do but fight their way blindly west. He ascertained that it was only thirty miles across, but it took them eight days, for the area was rocky, grown up with a thick mat of blackjack and brush, and cut in all directions with great gullies that were impassable until the banks were cut down—and even then a hundred men would have to hold back the wagons with ropes as they descended, and as many as forty mules were used to pull them up the other side.

It was a backbreaking job for giants, and in that time of testing Hermenijildo proved his right to stand up and be counted with the men. His strength, his calmness, his quick perceptions, his ability to handle the men were qualities that made him stand out among his fellows, most of whom were putting forth Herculean efforts of their own.

Josefina ground corn at every stop until Ross had to tell her to take a rest. But Andrés had lapsed into a lethargy which made him useless.

On a particularly hard day they had trouble getting a heavily loaded wagon up the side of a gully. Hermenijildo had hitched up forty-four mules, and men walked alongside with ropes to keep the wagon from turning over. Still the wagon seemed to be held back with invisible chains. Ross rode alongside.

"You ask me," he said, "I don't think those axles are greased. They act like they're plugged up with mud and sand." He wiped the sweat from under his hatband. He pointed forward. "The lead chain is digging into the edge of the ground up there. But hell—forty-four mules ought to be able to pull Fort Towson across the Red River. We broke two doubletrees and a hound on this wagon already, so it isn't the mules' fault." Ross made a decision. "Tell the men to tie their ropes to the axles and running gear and fasten the wagon to the trees. We'll jack up a wheel and see what it looks like."

They got the end of the wagon raised. The wheel was fast on the axle and they had to pry it off, turning and pulling. Ross looked up and saw Andrés at the edge of the crowd, watching. Ross turned hard. "You haven't greased this axle since we left Fort Towson," he said.

"*Señor,* the mud—"

"It was your job," Ross said implacably.

Andrés' eyes dropped. "I'm sorry, *señor.*"

Ross had a moment of pity for him, then told Her-menijildo: "You will be in full charge of the wagons from now on—both maintenance and moving. We'll try to stop early tonight to organize crews and take care of every wagon. There must be no more of this pulling against ourselves."

Apolinar was still in charge of hunting, and had become very good at it. Tapia kept scouting parties ahead and behind, for they had come upon abandoned villages and knew that Indians were in the area. Ross took charge of a party to make a trail through the trees and brush; the growth was so thick there was no way of accomplishing this except by cutting down trees with axes; stones too high to clear the axles of the wagons had to be broken up or moved.

Hermenijildo kept the wagons moving, and there were times when he seemed to will them forward. But no longer did they think of progress in terms of miles per day; there were times when a hundred yards was all they could move in half a day.

Then, almost unbelievably, they broke through the western edge of the Cross Timbers and found dry, open prairie, with the sun warmly overhead, the limitless light blue sky stretching toward infinity in the west, and a soft spring breeze carrying the scent of the first wild flowers.

They stopped at a spring for two days, and Ross found a man who could blacksmith, impressed two men into service with him, had them set up a forge and go to work on the running-gear of the wagons. Tires were tightened, hubs banded, axles straightened, shoes applied to the leading mules—for unshod mules had difficulty with footing on green grass.

The prairies west of the Cross Timbers were a series of broad shelves, each one higher than the last. They would mount one plateau expecting to cross it and descend on the other side; there would be good traveling for two or three days; then they would reach an area of breaks—rough country—and after traversing that would find themselves on another plateau, higher than the last one.

Water was a problem, for the streams were largely brackish, loaded with mineral salts that made them not only unpalatable but unhealthful to both men and mules. In the absence of guides who knew springs, Ross himself rode far and wide every day in connection with Apolinar to spy out springs of fresh water or near-fresh water that would supply enough for the big train.

The great undulating prairies furnished good footing and excellent grazing; the mesquite grass was now luxuriant, and the mules made as much as thirty miles a day, and still fattened.

Then one midmorning Ross, with Hermenijildo at his side, sat the gelding atop a hill, looked below, and saw the well-marked trail made by the train on its way north. Ross looked at Hermenijildo and grinned. "*Hombre,*" he said, "we'll soon be back in Chihuahua, and you can find out whether it's a boy or a girl."

Hermenijildo smiled for the first time in days. "I have hope it will be a boy," he said. "My Chonita before I left decided to call him Felipe—in your honor, *señor.*"

For a moment Ross was embarrassed. "I—well, I'm sure I would be honored," he said at last.

They turned south and followed their own trail. Ross had hoped to run into their Tonkawa guides—Soft-Shelled Turtle and his companions—but day after day they crawled along under the blue Texas sky and the ever warmer sun without any indication of Indians.

Nevertheless Ross was worried. There were plenty of Indians in the country, he knew, and he began to feel they were holding off to let the train get deep into their territory before they made themselves known.

He issued repeated warnings to Tapia's men, and constantly urged none to go out of sight of the main body for any purpose. For all of them, he warned, the demands of modesty must now be subservient to self-preservation. He knew it was inevitable that most of the men would take his warnings lightly, but he hoped, by constant vigilance, to avoid a tragedy.

Andrés was now no more than a fat teamster with a long black mustache and a scraggly beard. He drove his team during the day, cooked his meal at night over a separate fire with Josefina, and kept his own counsel. Ross no longer asked him to sit in on discussions, but Andrés did not appear to mind. Nevertheless, as they continued south, a look of thoughtfulness appeared in his black eyes. It became a worried look as the train penetrated farther and farther into Comanche country, reaching for the Rio Grande, steadily cutting down the miles to Chihuahua. . . .

They were about three days north of the Pecos when the Comanches struck. It was early evening, and so still the distant barking of prairie dogs was plainly heard throughout the camp. The sound of Josefina grinding corn on the *metate* arose presently, but unnatural quiet pervaded the countryside to such an extent that Hermenijildo remarked about it.

"I don't doubt the Indians have been here ahead of us, probably driving off the game to force us to hunt them out and trade mules with them," Ross said.

Suddenly the entire camp was brought to its feet by an electrifying scream. One of Tapia's men rode into camp from his post at a hard gallop. "*¡Los indios! ¡Los indios!*" he called in a hoarse voice. Though he was no longer holding the reins, he somehow managed to retain his balance. His horse, with blood streaming down its hip from a lance wound, galloped past Ross; its reins were trailing. The man's hat was gone; one side of his head was a mass of bright blood, and his face was gray and contorted with pain. His shirt, torn open to the waist, revealed his chest covered with blood.

The horse stepped on a rein and went over on its neck, its hindquarters going far into the air from its momentum. At the top of the arc the man was thrown off. He fell in a huddle, face down and knees under him, an arrow projecting from his back.

Shots sounded in the direction from which he had come, and Ross barked at Tapia, who shouted orders at his men and ran for a mule. The soldier's horse was screaming piteously with a broken thighbone. Ross put a cap on his pistol, stepped up, and shot the horse in the ear.

Tapia's men were beginning to gallop toward the

sound of shooting, which now had stopped. Hermeni-jildo galloped up, leading the black gelding. Ross seized the reins. The soldier on the ground was dead. Ross vaulted into the saddle and shouted, and rode out after Tapia.

They had a surprisingly short distance to go. Andrés and four *arrieros* had gone over the hill with rifles and pistols, probably hunting. The Comanches had caught them not over four hundred yards from camp, and the carnage was frightful. How it had been done in a few seconds Ross did not know, but one of the men was dis-emboweled; two had had their hands cut off; one was almost beheaded; and Andrés—poor fat Andrés, who had lost all ambitions but one—was bristling with arrows in his abdomen; his face was crisscrossed with bloody knife slashes, and his chest had been opened and his heart torn out.

"Shall my men follow them?" asked Tapia.

"No!" thundered Ross. "Stay back and guard the train! There may be another party watching!"

"*Sí, señor.*"

Ross got down and examined the men's firearms. They had all been fired. Ross straightened up. "They fought back," he said, "and undoubtedly killed a few of the devils." He said to Hermenijildo, "Get a burial detail up here, with at least twenty armed men to guard them."

"*Sí, señor.*" Hermenijildo galloped back to the camp. Ross searched the ground, and by the time Hermeni-jildo returned, Ross had come to a conclusion. While the men were digging a common grave, Ross took Her-

214

menijildo and Apolinar to one side. "It's probably best this way," he said. "I think Don Mauricio will live more happily in the knowledge that his son died a hero than he would if Andrés had returned home fat and lazy. It may be that Andrés planned it this way—but that must not be repeated to anyone. Do you both understand me?"

They both nodded gravely. Not only had Hermenijildo turned sober during the past year; Apolinar had also acquired an air of maturity.

Ross studied them both. "There is other business at hand; perhaps Andrés has opened a way to take care of it. You remember Carlota?"

They both nodded vigorously.

"I owe my life to her and her husband," he said. "That is not, however, reason enough to risk the success of this entire expedition."

They watched him gravely.

"We are almost at the Pecos, and from there it is only a few days to Presidio. I think Plácido and Tapia could get the train there if they had to. The lieutenant has a good knowledge of the country and of the Indians, and certainly Plácido knows mules."

They both agreed.

"We may be able to rescue her. There is danger—"

"*Señor*," Hermenijildo said with feeling, "if there is anything we can do to save anyone from these bloodthirsty savages—"

Ross said thoughtfully, "The Comanches now have two big affairs to celebrate: the taking of scalps and the killing of some of their warriors."

215

"You think—"

"It's obvious those men didn't die with their hands in their pockets," said Ross. "Andrés' six-shooter had been fired four times."

Hermenijildo nodded.

"The Comanches will not expect us to leave the train and attack them, and I am sure they will give their full attention to celebrating these events. While they are doing that, they will be highly vulnerable. It may be we can slip into their camp and get the girl without a fight."

Apolinar said grimly, "*Señor,* if a fight is necessary—"

"I'm counting on you—but let's get one thing straight. One man must stay back and hold the horses. Hermenijildo, that will be you."

"*Señor—*"

"No argument. You are married. Also, you are very dependable. You won't get excited and do anything foolish. I will expect you to hold the horses. If anything happens to us, you will try to be reasonably sure whether we can reach you. If not, you are to return to the train at the Pecos—because the train will keep traveling, just in case the Comanches have a spy out."

"I don't—"

"Your black can outrun any horse the Comanches may have. It will be your duty to return."

"But, *señor,* they may torture—"

"It is not likely." Ross took a deep breath. "The Comanches kill very savagely sometimes, but generally they don't waste much time on it. I think you will soon know."

Apolinar said eagerly, "Then I go with you?"

Ross nodded and rode off to give instructions to Lieutenant Tapia.

"We are going to try to rescue the girl," said Ross. "If we do not come back, you are in charge. If Hermenijildo comes back, he will be in charge. Your duty is to get the train to Presidio by the same trail we made going to Arkansas."

"I will do that, *señor.*"

"Dr. Connelly will meet you in Presidio."

Tapia said fervently, "I hope you will return to us in good health, *señor.*"

Ross was moved. "*Gracias. Bien,* move out in the morning as usual. We'll try to join you at the Pecos tomorrow or next day. But keep moving!"

"*Sí, señor.*"

Tapia's acceptance of his charge made Ross feel better. The lieutenant had carried himself well for the entire trip, but he had not been thoroughly tested until now. Ross was pleased to note that the sudden responsibility did not seem to go to his head.

Ross saw Apolinar loading his rifle, and told the two young Mexicans: "Be sure you've all got rifles, six-shooters fully loaded—five shots anyway, and knives and tomahawks with you. If we have to fight we'll fight hard."

"I would not mind killing a few Comanches," said Apolinar, "but if we are engaged in a fight some of us will be killed, too."

"If my plan works," said Ross, "there won't be any fight."

217

"If it does not," Hermenijildo noted, "you'll end up like Andrés."

"Do you want to change your mind?" asked Ross. "There's no shame if you do. You have a child now." He was trying to make it easy for Hermenijildo.

"No, *señor,*" Hermenijildo said stoutly.

Chapter 18

As they went over the hill, Ross pointed out the course. He set the gelding into a lope, and the others followed. They reached the canyon with the sun shining in the western end as it had a year earlier. He found the path and led them down it. Dogs barked at them and scurried out of the way. Children ran to hide, and heavily built squaws stared from openings in their teepees.

The four men stayed close together, and none bothered them as they rode through the village, but Ross knew the path behind them was closed until Muke-war-rah should open it. He could not find the chief's tent, but abruptly Ish-a-ro-yeh appeared. "You want something?" he asked.

"We want to see Muke-war-rah."

"Muke-war-rah too busy make useless talk. You come back tomorrow."

"Not tomorrow," Ross said. "We have come to talk. We have goods to trade."

Ish-a-ro-yeh studied him for a moment, then said: "You follow me. Leave horses."

"We do not leave horses," Ross answered. "We will follow you."

Ish-a-ro-yeh gave no sign that he had heard. He turned and led them, in his awkward walk, to the right. They reached the big teepee with the buffalo painted on it, and there were the same men around the campfire, with Muke-war-rah of the big-boned, evil face and the strangely thin eyebrows, his black hair, braided, hanging down his left shoulder. He was sitting in front of his teepee, and he did not look up as the men rode to the fire.

Ross alighted. "Remember, do nothing unless I tell you."

"*¡Silencio!*" roared Muke-war-rah.

Ross calmly turned his reins over to Apolinar and went to the fire. "Are the great Muke-war-rah's ears so tender that he cannot endure the song of the curlew?" he asked.

The great face lifted and the evil eyes looked at him. "I said you leave your horses."

"Do you think I trust your young braves enough to leave my horses?" Ross took five sacks of tobacco out of his shirt and passed them around. Then, remembering Ish-a-ro-yeh, he gave another one to him.

"The Brown Beard," Muke-war-rah said shrewdly, "was here last year about this time. Is it then a custom to violate our hunting grounds?"

"We have not been back home," said Ross. "We are on our way now."

"I know," said Muke-war-rah. "You have many wagons, much goods. Last year you have few wagons, no goods. You would not trade."

"I am sure you know all about us," said Ross.

"We have watched you many days—before you turn south and leave the Red River. What you want now?"

"We want to trade."

Muke-war-rah shook his head. "Is not necessary. My men watch your train. We will get your goods at the Pecos."

"It is not likely," Ross said, squatting before the fire, his rifle on his thighs. "We have more men than last year."

"You tricked us last year," said Muke-war-rah in sudden anger.

Ross laughed. "You could have followed us."

Muke-war-rah scowled, and Ross was amused. He knew why the Comanches had not followed: when they discovered that the train had already crossed the Pecos, they had been confused and instinctively had turned to flight.

An old Comanche squaw waddled up to the fire with a towsack on her back, heavy with its contents. She swung it to the ground, grasped one ear, and upended the whole thing over the fire. A bushel of terrapins tumbled out and fell into the live coals, and instantly there was a mad scrambling of legs and a frantic stretching of necks as the terrapins felt the heat and made violent efforts to escape.

Muke-war-rah sat there with a stick, and whenever a terrapin escaped from the fire on his side he calmly put the stick under it and flipped it back into the fire. All the braves around the fire followed his example, and in a few moments there was a crackling and popping as the shells began to burst from the heat.

Ross, to hide his feelings, said, "There must be few buffalo if your people are reduced to eating terrapin."

Muke-war-rah watched the last live terrapin, its head seared and its eyes burned out by the fire, go around in a tight circle and then over and over, trying to escape the torture. Muke-war-rah snorted, then pushed the stick under the terrapin and tossed it back into the fire. "It will not make the price any lower," he said.

"We have goods this time," said Ross. "We can make a deal if you still have the captive."

Muke-war-rah studied him. "We have the woman. The child we had to kill. She whimpered. The woman—I have had to beat her many times with the lance. She is more stubborn than any mule. Maybe I will sell her to you, but the price will be high."

"There's no reason why it should be," said Ross, "if you don't like her any more."

"I like her—but I'm tired of getting my face scratched. I've beaten her until my arms are heavy, but still she fights."

Ross now asked the question he feared to have answered. "Let us see her."

Muke-war-rah scowled again, and Ross knew his fears were well founded. Muke-war-rah knew he would have to show the captive to make a trade, but he was reluctant to do so, and there could be only one reason: he had abused Carlota so much that even his primitive Indian mind was aware that her value was lower than it should be. "How much you give?" he demanded.

Ross said speculatively, "Two bolts of goods, very pretty; five pounds of tobacco—"

"Rifles!" Muke-war-rah said suddenly. "You give six rifles!"

"No rifles," said Ross. "If your young braves want rifles they can try to take them away from us—but I warn you, many Comanche souls will wander in blackness throughout eternity if they try."

Muke-war-rah grunted suddenly. His eyes were narrow. "You give one bolt of goods for every squaw in camp."

Ross tried to laugh convincingly. "No squaw is worth that much. Besides, you have not shown her to me yet." He had to know if she was there, what her condition was, and if she could travel.

Muke-war-rah arose. As before, his great size was breathtaking. He stamped to the teepee, went inside, and grunted in Comanche. Ross heard the girl answer, and then the bone-crushing impact of a big hand on her face. She came up screaming at the chief, and Ross began to understand why Muke-war-rah was willing to trade her off. Muke-war-rah was losing face with his own men for his inability to tame her. He would be glad to get rid of her.

Ross held his breath as the huge Indian dragged her out to the fire. For a moment he thought he would rise up and kill Muke-war-rah. The girl was thin to emaciation; they had been trying to starve her into submission. The left side of her face was swollen beyond all recognition, and one eye completely closed. Her arms were tied behind her, and her right leg was twisted. Her hair was uncombed, her skin dirty, her clothing in shreds.

"*Señora,*" Ross said gently, "we will try again. Please be patient."

The one eye stared at him and suddenly seemed to open wider. Ross realized that she had heard nothing but Comanche for over a year and had almost forgotten her own language. She tried to talk through swollen lips, but the words were unrecognizable. Muke-war-rah seized her and flung her back into the teepee.

When Ross was sure he could control his voice, he said, shaking his head: "You have beaten her too much. You don't expect a big price for a woman like that."

"She is a Mexican," Muke-war-rah replied. "Her people will give much to get her back."

"She has no people. Your braves killed them all."

Muke-war-rah grinned insolently at him. "You want trade?"

Ross nodded and got up casually. "Three bolts of cloth, three pounds tobacco, beads, vermillion. No more."

He waited, eyes half-closed.

Muke-war-rah said angrily, "I trade. You come back tomorrow."

Ross got up and faced Muke-war-rah. The chief was at least half a head taller than he was. "If you beat her more, the price will go down," he warned.

Muke-war-rah growled. Ross turned to his horse, sick at heart. He got on his horse and followed Ish-a-ro-yeh to the edge of the village. He gave him another sack of tobacco and trotted the gelding back up the path. Up on top, he stopped to give the horses a breather. Then he struck out on the return path.

"What now?" asked Hermenijildo.

"As soon as we're out of sight," said Ross, "we turn around and approach the canyon from the other side."

"Won't there be lookouts?" asked Hermenijildo.

"Not likely," said Ross. "Down in that canyon, I doubt if they ever post a lookout unless they have reason to expect an attack."

"Why don't we just trade for Carlota?" asked Apolinar anxiously.

"We won't get a chance. That raiding party will be back before we could deliver the goods, and once the Comanches start their wailing and mourning there'll be no trading of captives for a long time. It's quite possible they'll kill her anyway to vent their spleen." Ross stopped them. "We've passed the last lookout. They're posted to see that we get started back in the right direction; then they'll forget us and go off hunting. Meanwhile, we'll go down this *arroyada* here until we can cut across to the west. We'll camp on the other side tonight. At daylight we'll go back to Muke-war-rah's camp."

"Why not earlier?"

"If I guess right, that raiding party will send in a runner tomorrow morning with news of the casualties, and the whole camp will go out to meet the survivors. Then I think we'll have a chance."

The opportunity came about midmorning. While Ross and Apolinar were watching from the south rim, with Hermenijildo guarding their horses, grazing in a hollow where they were not easily seen, a Comanche warrior came in on a bareback paint pony and rode through the camp with a wailing howl that brought every resident to the opening of his teepee. Then at different spots in the village arose great wailings and moans of anguish as Comanche women cut off their hair and scarified their arms and legs and abdomens and ran naked through prickly pear cactus trees in mourning for lost husbands or sons. Presently a slow exodus began toward the east, and Ross told his companions what to do. "Hermenijildo will stay and hold the horses, for without them we cannot get out of this country alive. You, Apolinar, will follow me down that path into the canyon. Leave your hat up here. Single file and on foot, we look enough like Indians not to be noticed for a long time, especially since the Comanches will be occupied. Are you ready?"

"Let's go," said Apolinar.

Ross went down the path, and Apolinar followed at a ten-yard interval. He had picked out the chief's teepee by its design, and now they went straight to it. The village seemed deserted, but Ross was cautious. He walked quietly around the teepee on his moccasins and found an Indian sitting before the entrance. The Indian looked up; it was Ish-a-ro-yeh. He opened his mouth to yell, but Ross was on him like a wildcat. He buried his knife in the hollow in Ish-a-ro-yeh's leathery throat, and the warning yell bubbled and was drowned in the Indian's blood.

Ross jerked his knife and stepped inside. "Carlota," he said softly.

He heard no answer, no sound. As he grew accustomed to the dimness, he found her, thoroughly tied and gagged with rawhide strips and thrown on the bare dirt floor. He bent over her, sliced off the bonds and the gag, stood her on her feet to be sure she was alive, and then took her thin hand and led her outside. As she blinked in the sunlight, he glanced at her to see if she was in condition to walk. "Follow me," he whispered.

They went back the same way—not fast, for fear of attracting attention. Apolinar was behind them.

A young Comanche brave had tried to steal the horses. Hermenijildo had spotted him first and had waited beside the black. When the Comanche had reached out for the black's reins; Hermenijildo had slipped a knife into his heart.

Ross looked down. "You damn' near skinned him to get the scalp," he said, "but there's no time now for a lesson. *Señora*," he said to Carlota, "can you ride behind me?"

She nodded. She was unbelievably wild-looking and the odor of her body was repulsive, but none of them mentioned it. The important thing now was to get her back to civilization to give her a chance to recover from her year of brutality and terror.

They mounted. "If the Comanches look for us," said Ross, "they will make for our trail. Therefore we'll go straight south from here to the next canyon, and then head southeast to meet the train about the Pecos crossing."

"Won't Muke-war-rah try to get Carlota back?"

"Why should he?" Ross asked. "He was glad to get rid of her."

They swung around to the east after they had crossed

the canyon, met the Pecos, and followed it down. The water was much too high for fording, and Ross was worried. At noon of the second day, after hard riding, they found the well-marked trail of the caravan, and by evening they came upon the camp.

Ross delivered the girl to the care of Josefina, who, although horrified at her condition, set about to gather herbs and prepare medicines to help her recover.

Ross went off to look over the river.

"It's too high to cross," said Lieutenant Tapia, "without ruining the goods."

"We'll cross it anyway. Apolinar!"

"*Sí, señor.*"

"Gather up a dozen water kegs and empty them. Have them here in half an hour."

"*Señor,*" said Tapia, "surely you are not going to cross tonight."

Ross looked at him. "With a thousand Comanches over yonder in the canyon, do you think we should loiter, *Teniente?*"

Tapia was impressed—more specially when Ross promised him a bonus for having brought the train as far as he had.

By the light of torches they lashed empty kegs, with stopped bungholes, under the wagonbeds. They rolled these into the roily river, with a light on the far side to guide the mules, while men stood on the upriver side with ropes to be sure the loads did not turn over. When the first wagonload rolled out on the sand at the far side, Ross put men to work unlashing the empty kegs and taking them back across the river. Hermenijildo, meanwhile, had secured more kegs and was preparing the second wagon.

They were over before the sky began to turn gray above the mesquite and greasewood to the east.

Tapia said, "We rest now, *señor?*"

They would have, but Ross, having crossed the Pecos, now found himself filled with a new power and drive that he had not known before. "No, Lieutenant," he said. "It is best we go on. Another day's march will put us out of reach of the Comanches."

That day they drove the mules as only Mexicans could drive them. A mule was not broken in, said the *arrieros,* until his shoulder blades stuck through his skin.

A few days later they had slowed to a more reasonable pace, and Ross began to feel victory within his reach. Then, half a day from Presidio del Norte, after he had seen the mud huts of the town from the left bank of the Del Norte, he saw a furious cloud of dust coming up the trail and rode out to meet it.

The square form of Dr. Connelly emerged from the dust cloud, as Ross had half anticipated. He roared a glad welcome, and shook hands hard. "By God, you made it!" he said. "Any trouble?"

"Five men killed by Comanches," said Ross, "including Andrés."

"I'm sorry to hear it," said Connelly, and looked past him at the long line of wagons and mules. "It is a great thing you have done, Ross, to bring this huge train across wilderness country with no greater loss than that. But," he said soberly, "there is more trouble ahead."

"What?"

Connelly faced him. "Governor Irigoyen died two months ago. Conde has taken his place, and he has canceled the agreement we had with Irigoyen on the duties."

Chapter 19

R oss looked at him almost in disbelief. They rode in silence for a moment, and then Ross asked, "And Conde has raised the tax?"

"They demand so much in duties that we cannot afford to haul the goods to Chihuahua."

"You can't afford *not* to," said Ross.

"I have a bill of lading for all the goods, and I have tried to talk Conde into some concessions, but at present he is adamant."

"And there is nothing else we can do?"

"Not one damn' thing. The moment we take this train past Presidio without customs certificates, we are liable to confiscation."

"How much of this is influenced by Cordero?"

Connelly shrugged. "Quite a bit, perhaps—though Conde has never been partial to us, as you know."

Ross said abruptly, "Have you given up?"

"By no means," said Connelly, "though I don't know yet how much of a licking we'll take. We'll get the train into Presidio and keep trying to negotiate with Conde."

"Tell him," said Ross, "that I'll take it back to Arkansas before I'll pay full duties on it."

Connelly began to ride south with him. "It's a poor bluff and he'll know it, because most of the money was put up by Chihuahua merchants, and they'll have the final say."

Ross was silent a moment. "Hell of a note," he said finally.

Connelly was as glum as he was. They had spent a year, said Connelly, and they had made the trip but they had lost the opportunity. Any way they looked at it, the expedition could not possibly make any money, and it would take years to get together enough money to try again. "The merchants," said Connelly, "are not concerned with glory of achievement but with making a profit."

Ross took a deep breath. "What do we do now?"

"Cross the river and camp near Presidio del Norte, while I dicker with Don Lawreano and make weekly trips to Chihuahua to try to influence Conde."

Ross found out, as they waited at the Rio Grande for the train, that the expedition was closer to bankruptcy than Connelly had told him. High interest rates on the money, plus a soft market in Chihuahua because of heavy traffic on the Sante Fe Trail during the year they had been gone, meant that it was vital to get concessions from Conde just to break even.

"You have one bargaining position," Ross observed. "If you can make him believe you would turn it back into Texas—say Austin or San Antonio—before you would pay the full duty, then perhaps he would settle for half, to get so much cash in the treasury."

"That's what I've been working on. I've asked for

half but I don't think I'll get it. Whatever I do get will determine whether we lose money or break even."

"Since it doesn't help me either way," Ross noted, "I shouldn't give a damn how it comes out—but I do. This expedition is not finished until we roll into Chihuahua, and I intend to be at the head of it then."

"At least," Connelly noted, "you are protected by the sharp deal you made with us on the mules."

The first team came up, and Plácido took them into the Rio Grande. It was hardly hock-deep over the limestone bed, and the crossing was easy. Ross sent Hermenijildo to locate a campsite and arrange for grazing the animals. "It will cost money to stay here," he warned Connelly.

"I'll do *my* best. Meantime, try to keep your men out of trouble."

Ross smiled wryly. "Frankly, I have half a notion to let them tear the town apart and help them do it. Maybe Don Lawreano would plead our cause with Conde and get some allowances."

Connelly said: "I know how you feel, Ross. But you'll still get your fixed fee and the mules."

"All right," said Ross. "What's the important news from Chihuahua?"

Connelly faced him, his face emotionless, his eyes watchful. "It is said the Doña Valeria will marry Mangum in October."

Ross swallowed hard. "She's not yet married?" he asked then.

"No—but Don Fidel has issued his approval, as indeed he was practically forced to do."

Ross said, "I should have written her."

"From what the women say, it would have taken only a word from you to stop it—and perhaps it would do so yet. I would be pleased to take a message."

Ross took a deep breath. "I have my pride," he said. "Doña Valeria is a half-owner of Los Saucillos, and I had hoped to go to her with money of my own. But now I am not yet in Chihuahua." He stared toward Chihuahua. "It is hard suddenly to want money so very much and to have none."

They settled down in camp, and Ross went first to see how Carlota was. He was astonished to discover how quickly she had filled out and regained her natural prettiness. She limped a little, and she had many small scars on her arms and legs, but she had washed and combed her hair to a glossy black, and her skin was scrubbed until it was dusky only in the hollows, and the light was back in her eyes as he had seen it in Chihuahua.

"*Señora*," he said. "I am tremendously happy to find you improving."

She smiled. "*Gracias, señor.*"

"Do you have parents in Presidio—brothers, sisters? Any relatives?"

"I have a sister who works for Don Fidel at Los Saucillos."

"That's good."

"Perhaps I can get work at the *rancho*. If I could go to Chihuahua with you, *Señor*—"

"You certainly may," he said. She was young and pretty and hardly older than Valeria, and she had

232

tremendous resilience of spirit to have endured the death of all her family and a year's brutality at the hands of Muke-war-rah, and still be able to smile after a few days' time. He thought she would make a fine wife for someone.

They stayed at Presidio for a month. Ross kept the teamsters on the payroll, thinking constantly that they would be going in a day or two, and not willing to break up the train to save a few hundred dollars.

Connelly was back and forth once a week, but it was not until the fifth trip that he announced, somewhat ruefully, that they had finally made a deal with Conde. He had compromised at duties of $300,000—no less, and they had been forced to pay it. With adroit juggling they would be able to break even on the venture.

And so once again the packs were laid in a long line and the mules sent to find their own places and stand until the packs were lashed.

Presently the big train was under way. Connelly, with the precious certificates stowed within his shirt, rode alongside Ross.

Ross stopped to watch the entire train pass by, and then galloped forward to Plácido, near the front. "Where's Josefina?" he asked.

Plácido's big face was sad. "She stay in Presidio with Santiago," he said. "But don' worry—she come back to Plácido!"

They crossed the dry, sandy desert of mesquite and ocotillo and beargrass and prickly pear. They made their camps without water and went on. Chihuahua came closer every day, and tension began to build in

Ross. It was September twentieth; only a few days more and the long trip would be over. . . .

They approached Chihuahua from the north. The mountain peaks to the west glowed with the last light of the setting sun, and the plain below them, covered with mesquite, lay in a golden shadow cast by the mountains. Quail piped as they called their coveys together for the night; jackrabbits cautiously left their cover in the brush. The lowing of cattle from the canals where they were being watered, the barking of dogs and sounds of children calling to one another, and the clapping of hands shaping tortillas for the evening meal all formed a subtle symphony of Mexican sounds.

But Ross was thinking of the trip. His share of the profits was exactly nothing. But he would have his fee and the mules. While not a fortune, it was a sizable sum.

Magoffin and Don Fidel met them at the gates, and Hermenijildo's grandfather and Dr. Jennison, and there was much shaking of hands and embracing in the Mexican fashion.

Ross went on to superintend the unloading of the mules, the placing of the wagons around the plaza, the disposition of the mules. To each man he gave a peso; they would not be paid off until the wagons were unloaded, and then they would receive their money in full. Meanwhile he had made arrangements for board and room for all who did not live in Chihuahua, and he asked only that they not get so drunk they would be unable to finish the job. There was grumbiing at this, but some recognized the justice of it, and all knew it would result in stretching the period of celebration.

They spent three days unloading the wagons and storing the goods in Connelly's and Magoffin's warehouses. Then Connelly took the wagons and the mules to Los Saucillos to await whatever future sale they could work out. That night Connelly, Magoffin, Don Fidel, Apolinar, Don Mauricio, Hermenijildo, and Ross sat down in Don Fidel's salon for a glass of brandy. Magoffin watched him pour. "New stuff?" he asked.

Don Fidel looked up. "I am ashamed to confess I suspect this was brought down the Trail by Cordero's men. However—" He held up the bottle. "It's real cognac, smooth as silk."

"If its qualities are what I remember, I'll forget that it was brought in by a competitor." Magoffin sipped the cognac and nodded, a pleased expression on his face. "This is very nearly as good as bourbon, Don Fidel."

Don Fidel glared at him, his great black mustaches bristling. "¡*Hombre!* You offer insult to the mules that hauled this nectar from St. Louis!"

Magoffin grinned and handed back his glass. "I may change my mind on a second sampling."

Don Mauricio was silent, but after his third glass he said thickly, "I am not blame you, Don Felip, for what happen to Andrés, but you will know it is a hard blow for a man to lose his only son."

"And yet," Connelly said judiciously, "It is better to lose him in the process of being a man—if one has to lose him."

Ross saw Apolinar's eyes on him, and turned away, remembering his words to Apolinar and Hermenijildo when they had found Andrés' body. He knew that none of them would ever say anything to disillusion Don Mauricio. He sampled his third glass of cognac. "He died facing the Comanches," he said, "and his six-shooter was empty. He fought like a tiger until they struck him down."

Don Mauricio's eyes, sunken a little in his fat face, showed his gratitude. He drained his fourth glass and got up. "If you gentlemen will excuse me," he said, and bowed and went out slowly, an old man.

"Will he be able to get home all right?" asked Ross.

Don Fidel nodded. "I gave my servant orders to accompany him."

None mentioned the tears brimming in Don Mauricio's eyes. It would be a hard night for him. . . .

"By God!" said Magoffin a half-hour later. "It's actually one of the greatest accomplishments in trail history." He struck his big knee with a ham-like hand. "In all my time on the Santa Fe Trail I never saw anything like it. A third of a million dollars—first through the Comanches as bullion, then back through the Comanches as goods—and you never lost a nickel's worth. Nothing like it was ever seen in this country—yet the feat will be lost to history because it didn't make money."

"If we had made money," Connelly agreed, "the trail would be swarming with wagons now, and the name of Ross Phillips would be known to our grandchildren. As it is—" He shrugged.

Ross got up. "Well, gentlemen, we had our fling—and right now I think I'm beginning to let down. I feel tired for the first time."

"There's no rush," said Don Fidel. "Your room is ready upstairs."

Ross glanced at him. "That's kind of you."

Connelly said wryly: "The whole town is talking about the deal you pulled on the mules. You must have expected something like this."

"I've traded in Mexico long enough to know it could happen—and so have you."

He rode around with Don Fidel the next morning, looking absently at the thousands of black horses, sorted into various divisions of the ranch according to age and sex. Don Fidel raised nothing else. Father Ramón was watering his nasturtiums as he had been doing in April of 1839—it was now late September of 1840—and he came over to offer congratulations on the success of the expedition.

That afternoon Ross went into town and settled up with Connelly and Magoffin. He got to Magoffin's warehouse to find the gray-haired *alcalde* there. "*Señor,* I am very sad to have done what I did to you," the *alcalde* said.

Ross stared at him, then looked at Connelly and Magoffin. He saw something wrong in their faces. "What is it?" he demanded.

Magoffin drew a deep breath. "The mules," he said, and stopped.

"What about the mules?" Ross asked in a hard voice.

"Complaint has been made to the governor that you took silver bullion out of Mexico without a permit, and your mules have been attached as security for payment of the export duty."

Ross studied him a moment, his mouth tight. "Mangum signed the complaint, I take it."

"Yes. He stands to get a per centage as informer, it is said."

Ross looked from one to another. "It seems there is only one way to take care of Mangum."

Chapter 20

Ross went to the Nine Cats. Some of his Arkansas teamsters were there. One borrowed a dollar from him; the others still had some money. He bought a round of pulque but did not join in the loud talk and banter and reminiscences of the trail. He sat soberly tasting the drink, and for the first time it made him feel revulsion. "It's not fresh," he told the proprietor. "It smells like putrid meat—*old* putrid meat."

The man threw up his hands in pretended horror. "*¡Señor!* This fine pulque was made only yesterday! I myself have seen the *licor divino* taken from the maguey. *Señor,* I cannot express to you—"

"All right," Ross said, and threw out a peso. "Bring me another."

The teamsters went out, inviting him to accompany them, but he declined. He sat at the little table and drank steadily. He had made the trip for one purpose: to acquire a competence to lay at the feet of Doña Valeria.

This time was different from all the other times

when he had completed a difficult mission. Always before he had had a glorious feeling of accomplishment, and in his elation it had seemed appropriate to throw away his money and look for the next challenge. But this one was different; he seemed somehow to have come to the end of something; the accomplishment was his and he was ready to enjoy the fruits of it—but there were no fruits; and he had no desire to go on a fling and throw away the money. Hell of a thing! he told himself.

More of the teamsters drifted in. Ross greeted them and bought them drinks but took no part in their amusements. For the first time in his life he was drinking himself into sadness. He knew it but he didn't care.

At some time during the night the door opened, the night breeze from the mountains flickered the lamps, and Josefina stepped inside and looked around uncertainly. One of the teamsters recognized her and called to her. She looked at him but did not answer. Then she saw Ross, and smiled shyly. He sat up straight and she came over.

His voice was thick. "How'd you get here?"

"I came by mule train—this evening, *señor.*"

"Pulque!" roared Ross. "Pulque for Josefina!"

She stood close to him.

"What happened to Santiago?" he asked.

"He got drunk," she said, "and did not come home one night. Another *hombre* came, and I was just talking to him, but there was no light, and—" She shrugged. "He was most jealous. He turns me out in the street, and I have decide' to come back home."

Ross grunted. "Plácido was right, wasn't he?"

Her eyes widened as she put a slim hand on his shoulder. "I have not seen Plácido," she said.

"You will. But in the meantime—"

"Yes, *señor?*"

Her lips were on his. Her arms went around his neck. "*¡Señor!*" she said in a husky whisper.

"Josefina!"

It was a harsh voice—one that Ross had heard few times, but one which, even though he had been drinking, he recognized immediately. He lifted the girl and twisted to stare at the door and the black-browed countenance of Ed Mangum.

Ross got to his feet without touching anything with his hands. His head cleared as he arose. He saw the look of jealousy on Mangum's face.

After Mangum's first glance at Josefina, his blazing eyes settled on Ross, and Ross knew that Mangum, too, had been drinking.

Ross had no weapon, but he saw Mangum's hand move toward his coat front. He froze Mangum's movement for an instant with a pointed forefinger. "You had a free shot at me already. Are you taking another?"

Mangum debated for only an instant. Then his thin veneer of Spanish gentility was swept aside completely. He drew the pistol as Ross leaped. The bullet grazed Ross's shoulder; then he closed with Mangum and, seizing the pistol with both hands, tore it from his grasp. As Mangum reached for a knife, Ross brought the barrel of the pistol down on Mangum's head. Again and again and again.

Ross felt a hand on his arm, and heard Magoffin's

voice: "Come along with us."

Magoffin took him to Connelly's place, where Dr. Jennison cleaned the wound with alcohol and put a bandage on it.

Ross felt the sting of the alcohol and thought of the many fights he had gone through in a year and a half—all for one purpose: to defeat Cordero. And now he had breached all the levels below Cordero, and only Cordero himself was left. Perhaps it would be a good thing to make a clean job of it. . . .

Magoffin was back the next morning. "Mangum died," he said, "but you're in the clear. There were several muleskinner witnesses, and they all say he drew on you without warning."

Dr. Jennison came back, beaming. "Good news—for you, at least," he told Ross. "Now that Mangum is dead, Conde is a little afraid of you. Since he has heard you intend to invest your money in Chihuahua anyway, it gives him a good excuse, and he has decided to release the attachment on the mules."

Ross smiled slowly. He shook hands with Jennison and then with Connelly and Magoffin. "It's too bad," he said to the latter, "that you can't swing some such club of your own."

Connelly poured more brandy.

"There's other good news too," said Magoffin. "This morning we talked the *alcalde* into remitting the bail money—since you actually returned."

Ross shook his head. "You're trying to give me ten thousand dollars."

"No, we merely threatened to throw our goods on

the market at half of Cordero's price, and since he has a train due here in a few days . . ." He chuckled. "Anyway, you get your fixed fee."

Ross grinned. "That's better than contributing it to the public coffers."

"Now," said Magoffin, "maybe you can propose to Valeria and my wife will quit pestering me about it."

"There's no question of money now," Connelly reminded him.

Ross looked at them. "Since my feeling about Valeria seems to be a prime topic of conversation in Chihuahua—"

"You needn't be sarcastic," said Connelly. "This is customary in Mexico."

"Very well, *amigos*—but consider this: I kill her fiancé: am I then immediately to propose marriage in his place?"

"My God!" said Connelly. "You certainly got it bad. I never saw such a touchy rooster."

Ross thought about it while he helped to dispose of the mules and wagons.

Adolf Speyer came in from Santa Fe after a bad trip across the desert and bought thirty of their wagons and three hundred mules to make the trip on to Mexico, and gave Ross a check for $36,000. Apolinar found Ross quietly having a cognac at the Nine Cats. Ross told Apolinar that he felt reasonably safe there, for Josefina had attached herself to one of the Arkansas teamsters who had gone on with Speyer's train.

Apolinar sniffed Ross's cognac. "I never knew Antonio to have anything like this before," he said.

"He didn't," said Ross, "until I cadged a bottle from Connelly and told him to keep it for me."

"Papá wishes to see you, *señor.*"

Ross downed the cognac. "Do you know why?"

"*Sí,* Papá wishes to offer you a partnership in Los Saucillos."

Ross laughed. "You're quizzing me."

"No, *señor,* I am quite serious. The *rancho* is much too big for one man."

"He has you."

"I have told him I would like to have you there."

"But—"

"The ranch is very big, *señor.* We do not know how many *varas*—millions, undoubtedly. And we have almost fifty thousand black horses—fifty thousand!"

Ross looked at him seriously. "That's a lot of horses," he agreed.

"You will talk about it?" urged Apolinar.

"If it's agreeable with you."

"I would be honored. Of course you understand, *señor,* that this is not a full partnership. It is in relation to what you can put into it."

"Of course."

"Then let us get out to the *rancho.*"

It was a pleasant ride in the warm sun, and overhead a caracara circled endlessly, looking for an unwary jackrabbit. "Nice country," said Ross, looking at the mountains.

"*Muy bonito,*" Apolinar agreed. "But always dry."

Don Fidel met them and led them past the barking dogs, past Father Ramón, past the staring black eyes of children.

He asked Peralta if he had found who tampered with the pistol before the duel.

"A girl named Anita, who took care of your room. She was bribed by Mangum. How—" He shrugged. "Anyway, Carlota's sister saw her, and told Carlota and Diego. Then Diego became very excited and borrowed one of my black geldings to gallop to Chihuahua. I found all this out later."

"Where is Anita now?"

"She went up the Trail with Mangum last summer and did not return. There are reports she is working in St. Louis."

They sat down with a glass of brandy.

"You like my proposition?" Peralta asked Ross.

"I like it if it isn't a gift."

"It is no gift. As you can well imagine, there is room for a good man at Los Saucillos. This is almost a state in itself."

"My money won't make much of a splash in this pond."

"Quite the contrary," said Don Fidel. "To be frank, I lost heavily on the Arkansas expedition. I'm not—'broken,' as you say, but I lack cash, and it will be a squeeze to operate the ranch until the colt crop comes along next spring, unless I can sell an interest to someone. And at the moment, *señor*, you have the only cash in Chihuahua."

"How is that? Surely Cordero—"

"His last train was attacked by Pawnees; many men were killed, much goods taken. Cordero is now no better off than the rest of us."

Ross said thoughtfully, "It sounds like a chance that does not come very often."

"Next year," Peralta agreed, "it may be much different."

Ross said, "Very well. Count on me."

"*¡Bien, señor! ¡Muy bien!* There is, of course, my other partner to be consulted, but I do not anticipate any difficulty."

"Your other partner?" asked Ross.

Peralta bowed low. "Señorita Doña Valeria Sierra," he said.

Ross was thunderstruck for a moment. "Am I to be—"

Apolinar said softly, "*Señor,* there is also a time to forget pride."

Ross stared at him, then smiled. "I guess you're right." He turned to Peralta. "Don Fidel, you are the legal guardian of the *señorita,* are you not?"

"Yes."

"Then I shall observe the proprieties by asking you for the hand of Doña Valeria in marriage."

Peralta started to smile, but checked it. "Very good, *señor,*" he said formally. "I shall take your request under consideration."

Before the round of social events got under way, a small family *tertulia* was held at which relatives, servants, and even the peons were welcomed. "It is an old Peralta custom," Don Fidel told Ross. And on the evening of the party, Don Fidel put an arm around Ross and another around Valeria and led them to the patio. "A present," he said, pointing, "from Don José Cordero."

Ross shook his head. "Two beautiful chestnut stallions! How is this possible?"

Don Fidel shrugged. "It is the way we do business. Cordero tried hard to defeat you, but there was nothing personal involved, and this is his apology to you."

"Well," said Ross, drawing a deep breath, "considering the number of times his men tried to kill me—" He broke off, then stole a glance at Valeria, for he thought she had been covertly watching him. So far their engagement had been extremely formal, and he had not been alone with her even to talk. It seemed that the closer he got to the screen of her Spanish fan, the greater the barrier there was between them.

"We have another surprise," said Don Fidel. "Hermenijildo!"

The tall young Mexican came into the room, and Ross shook hands. "You're going to let the mustache grow, I take it."

"*Sí, señor.*" He stepped aside to reveal the pretty Chonita, who held a bundle in her arms.

Ross laughed. "A boy or a girl, Hermenijildo?"

Chonita smiled and pulled back the blanket. "Felipe!" she said proudly.

Ross turned. "Don Fidel!" he cried. "Cigars!"

They danced, and Ross had only one objection: he didn't get a chance to dance with Valeria, for the girls of the ranch were allowed to claim him whenever they wished—and, it seemed, they wished. Before long he found himself dancing with a very pretty girl, handsomely dressed, who, like Chonita, also watched him as if amused.

"*Señorita,*" he said, "I know it is my evening to be laughed at, but do you mind telling me what is funny?"

She asked, and her voice was familiar—"Don't you know me?"

"Carlota!"

In his pleasure at seeing her well and pretty again, he hugged her. She was soft and yet pleasantly firm, like Valeria.

"*Señor*"—her eyes were searching his face—"are you about to tell me that I have ribs like a haunch of mutton?"

He stared at her for an instant, then looked up. Every woman in the room was watching him. He caught Valeria's eyes, and knew she had put Carlota up to it.

Slowly, his arm dropped from around Carlota and he turned toward Valeria and started to walk toward her. Then uncertain, and a little embarrassed, he stopped in the center of the floor.

It was deep twilight now; outside, in the patio, the doves went "*Cú, cú, cú.*" The gracious evening was very quiet and peaceful, and for a moment only the girlish laughter of a child was superimposed upon the clapping of brown hands shaping tortillas.

Then he was walking toward Valeria again through a bright mist of uncertainty. He stopped before her. "*Señorita, I—*"

As her arms went around him, he kissed her warm lips. Presently she drew back, her dark eyes on his.

"*Señor*, don't you hear? The music has stopped."

Ross held her a little way from him and shook his head slowly. "*Señorita*," he said earnestly, "the music has barely begun."

Center Point Publishing
600 Brooks Road • PO Box 1
Thorndike ME 04986-0001 USA

(207) 568-3717

US & Canada:
1 800 929-9108